Emily Harvale lives in East Sussex, in the UK –
although she would prefer to live in the French
Alps…or Canada…or anywhere that has several
months of snow. Emily loves snow almost as much
as she loves Christmas.

Having worked in the City (London) for several
years, Emily returned to her home town of
Hastings where she spends her days writing. And
wondering if it will snow.

You can contact her via her website, Twitter,
Facebook or Instagram.

There is also a Facebook group where fans can
chat with Emily about her books, her writing day
and life in general. Details are on the 'For You'
page of Emily's website.

Author contacts:
www.emilyharvale.com
www.twitter.com/emilyharvale
www.facebook.com/emilyharvalewriter
www.instagram.com/emilyharvale

***

Scan the code above to see all Emily's books on Amazon

Also by this author:

Highland Fling
Lizzie Marshall's Wedding
The Golf Widows' Club
Sailing Solo
Carole Singer's Christmas
Christmas Wishes – Two short stories
A Slippery Slope
The Perfect Christmas Plan – A novella
Be Mine – A novella
···

The Goldebury Bay series:
Book One – Ninety Days of Summer
Book Two – Ninety Steps to Summerhill
Book Three – Ninety Days to Christmas
···

The Hideaway Down series:
Book One – A Christmas Hideaway
Book Two – Catch A Falling Star
Book Three – Walking on Sunshine
Book Four – Dancing in the Rain
···

Hall's Cross series
Deck the Halls
The Starlight Ball
···

Michaelmas Bay series
Christmas Secrets in Snowflake Cove
Blame it on the Moonlight
···

Lily Pond Lane series
The Cottage on Lily Pond Lane – Book One
The Cottage on Lily Pond Lane – Book Two

Christmas

on

Lily Pond Lane

Emily Harvale

ISBN 978-1-909917-36-1

Published by Crescent Gate Publishing

Print edition published worldwide 2018
E-edition published worldwide 2018

Editor Christina Harkness

Cover design by JR, Luke Brabants and Emily Harvale

For Mattie.
And for all the brave and courageous women in
this world.

Acknowledgements

My grateful thanks go to the following:

Christina Harkness for her patience and care in editing this book.
My webmaster, David Cleworth who does so much more than website stuff.
My cover design team, JR.
Luke Brabants. Luke is a talented artist and can be found at: www.lukebrabants.com
My wonderful friends for their friendship and love. You know I love you all.
All the fabulous members of my Readers' Club. You help and support me in so many ways and I am truly grateful for your ongoing friendship. I wouldn't be where I am today without you.
My Twitter and Facebook friends, and fans of my Facebook author page. It's great to chat with you. You help to keep me (relatively) sane!
Thank you for buying this book.

Christmas

on

Lily Pond Lane

Chapter One

'No, Jet. Not there. To the left a bit. Up a fraction. Yes. That's it.' Mia Ward brushed a wayward lock of golden-brown hair from her cheek, smiled up at her boyfriend and sighed contentedly. 'That's perfect. Now make sure it doesn't fall off.'

Jet Cross raised an eyebrow, shook his head and grinned. 'You could do it yourself, you know.'

Mia grinned back as she tucked her scarf, decorated with snowmen, beneath the upturned collar of her cashmere coat. 'No thanks. You and Gill are doing a good job. What do you think, Ella?'

Mia's best friend, Ella Swann walked towards her across the crisp, frost-covered front lawn. She was carrying a tray with four mugs of coffee, and four iced cinnamon swirls that Mia had bought earlier from Lake's Bakes, which was just across the village green, on the other side of the pond.

1

Ella glanced up at the roof of Sunbeam Cottage and grinned mischievously. 'Are you sure the roof is strong enough to hold that lot?'

Mia tutted. 'That's exactly what Jet and Gill said when I sent them up there. But you were the one who wanted the four reindeer. I would've been happy with just the snowman and the coloured lights.'

'Is that coffee?' Ella's boyfriend Guillaume asked. 'Does that mean we can come down? It's freezing up here.'

'Hold on for one more second, Gill.' Mia stepped farther back to get a better view.

Jet and Gill were balanced precariously on the thatched roof, where they'd been for the last hour, fixing coloured fairy lights around the roof soffits and placing four large reindeer made from interwoven twigs by a local craftsman, and an even larger, plastic snowman, into the perfect positions. Mia had changed her mind several times on what the perfect positions were.

'I'm not sure we've got enough decorations,' Ella said, laughing. 'We want to make sure we're got the most decorated cottage in Little Pondale. Stay there while we find some more.'

'In your dreams,' Jet replied. 'We're coming down. Okay?' He glanced at Mia and she nodded.

'Yeah. You can come down. I'm happy.'

She was happy. Exceedingly happy. She'd been so since Halloween, the night Jet Cross had told her he loved her. The night they'd slept together for the very first time. The night she knew that, barring falling foul of the curse of Frog's Hollow, or any other unforeseen accidents, she would be ecstatically happy for the rest of her life.

She still couldn't believe it. So much had happened this year and it seemed incredible that she had only lived in the tiny, seaside village of Little Pondale since May, when she, Ella and Ella's twin brother, Garrick had moved into Sunbeam Cottage; the cottage she'd inherited from her – at the time unknown – great-aunt. Garrick had long since left, having returned to Scotland to be with his previous girlfriend and mother to be, Fiona. It was only after Mia had found happiness with Jet that she could bring herself to think of Garrick without a twinge of sadness. And she definitely had found happiness with Jet. Happiness and joy beyond her wildest dreams. Which was exactly what the fortune-teller at the Summer Fête had predicted. Virtually everything that woman had foretold had come to pass. Justin Lake, the former owner of the bakery had become an instant success in Hollywood in spite of the fact that his film wasn't even out yet. Ella and Gill were now quite clearly head over heels about each other, and Lori, Mia's mum, was happily living with her hunky Texan, Franklin in a cottage on Little Pond Farm.

The months Mia and Ella had spent in Little Pondale hadn't all been happy: Garrick leaving. The threats Mia had received. The lies and the betrayals. The attempts on Jet's life. Even now, the former vicar, Tom Tyburn was awaiting trial for that, and also for embezzling church funds, while his girlfriend, Alexia Bywater had already been tried for obstruction and assaulting a police officer. She was given one month's imprisonment and a £2,000 fine and would be released within the next few days, but no one expected her to re-join her family in the village pub, The Frog and Lily. Her brother Toby had mentioned to Mia and Jet that his parents were thinking of spending the holidays with a relative in Spain because his mum was desperate to be reunited with her daughter, despite the awful things Alexia had said and done, and Alexia had made it clear she wanted to get away from England for a time.

Yes, quite a lot had happened since Mia had moved to Little Pondale. Not only had she inherited Sunbeam Cottage, she'd also inherited her great-aunt's entire estate. The solicitor was still tying up loose ends and finalising matters, but he had confirmed that Corner Cottage, the blue-painted, thatched cottage at the beginning of Lily Pond Lane, also belonged to Mia. She'd offered it to her mum and Franklin, but Lori had said they were happy where they were. Ella and Gill had said the same.

'Why not rent it out for Christmas?' Ella suggested as soon as it officially became Mia's in early December. 'It's a shame to leave it empty but I think it's a bit too soon for me and Gill to

4

actually move in together. At least living here, we have separate rooms, even if we do only use mine. Besides, if Gill moved out, you'd have no one to cook for you.'

'That's a very good point. I hadn't thought of that.' Mia had never really learnt to cook. Nor had Ella, come to that. It wasn't something either of them particularly enjoyed. Mia still couldn't see what was so wrong about eating pizza, or ding dinners (microwaveable ready meals) each night. For some reason, Gill considered the microwave to be an instrument of evil, and the only pizza he would eat was one he'd made from scratch.

After discussing with Jet what she should do about Corner Cottage, Mia decided to take Ella's suggestion and rent it out. Fred Turner, who had recently married Hettie Burnstall, Mia's elderly friend and cleaning lady, was a whizz with technology, despite the fact he was in his early eighties. He'd put together a website to advertise the cottage and within two days, enquiries and phone calls had come flooding in. Several people had been put off when they were told that, yes, it was correct that mobile phone reception was non-existent in the village – unless you climbed the three hundred steps in the church steeple, or went to the very top of Frog Hill. A few more balked at the prospect of staying in a village with only one pub and no shops except a small bakery, and Little Pond Farm, which sold fresh milk, freshly laid eggs, and handmade butter and cheese. One or two were astonished that the cottage had no TV. Why these people bothered to phone Mia's landline, or send her emails to check these things when it was made clear on the website, was beyond her. But one person said they'd called to check because "in this day and age, it was incomprehensible that a rental property should be so lacking in basic necessities". That made Mia laugh, but she remembered how shocked she and Ella had been when they'd discovered that Sunbeam Cottage had no TV. Grace Tyburn, the former owner of Corner Cottage had clearly felt the same about TV as had Mia's great-aunt, Mattie. But then Grace had lost a fortune on online gambling. Broadband was one thing nearly every cottage had, and since fibre optic had recently been installed, one or two had very fast connections. Not Corner Cottage though and not Sunbeam Cottage either. Mia had meant to get it upgraded, but she hadn't got around to it. Despite all the apparent 'issues' with Corner Cottage, someone had finally said that it was perfect. Exactly what they were looking for. And they would be arriving this week.

Mia took a mug of coffee and a cinnamon swirl from Ella's tray and offered them to Jet the moment he stepped off the ladder onto the frost-covered ground. Instead of taking them, he wrapped his arms around her and kissed her. She almost spilt the coffee but she managed to keep the mug fairly level as she savoured his kiss. Until he pressed a cold hand against her cheek.

'God, Jet! Your hand's freezing. And now you've made me spill your coffee.'

He gave her a cheeky grin and grabbed another mug from the tray Ella held towards him and Gill.

'Your coffee,' Jet said, winking at Mia. 'I'm having this one. I just wanted you to know how cold it was up there. But because I love you, I'd brave arctic conditions to make you happy.'

Ella laughed and rolled her eyes. 'Does he think that scores him extra Brownie points?'

'It does,' Mia said, smilingly lovingly at Jet before taking a bite of the cinnamon swirl. 'Wow. This is delicious. I know we all thought we'd miss Justin's buns when he left, but I'm beginning to think it was a good thing he went. Jenny's buns are even better.' Jenny Lake was Justin's cousin and she had renamed the bakery, Lake's Bakes when she'd taken over in November.

'I know it was a good thing,' Gill said, kissing Ella as he took his coffee and cake. 'If he hadn't, Ella might still be with him instead of going out with me.'

'Aww.' Ella grinned and tossed the now empty tray on the white-tipped grass. 'Isn't this sweet? We're all loved up and getting ready to spend our first Christmas together.'

'I can't believe it's only just over one week away,' Mia said. 'I think we should put some decorations up at Corner Cottage later today. Not quite as many as we've got here. Just some lights and stuff.'

She glanced up at the reindeers and snowman on the roof and then down to the row of colourful fairy lights; down farther to the holly wreath on the front door and the row of light-up, red and white striped candy canes running along the length of the path. The inflatable snowman stood proud on the front lawn to her left as did the gorgeous Norway Spruce tree to her right, decorated with frost-proof lights and baubles. It was possible that she and Ella had gone a tad overboard. But hey. They both loved Christmas and they were happy. That was reason enough to go a bit OTT.

'So you want me and Gill to clamber over another roof?' Jet asked, giving her a rather sexy, sideways glance. 'That's going to cost you.'

'I'll happily pay any price.' She winked at him and returned his suggestive grin. 'I only want a few lights on the roof. And possibly some of these light-up candy canes. I'd like it to look festive when the Hardmans arrive but perhaps not quite as festive as this.'

'And a snowman,' Ella said. 'You've got to give them a snowman. Kids love snowmen.' She gave Mia a questioning look. 'Did you say Hardmans?'

'Kids?' Mia said at the same time. 'I didn't know they were bringing kids. They told me it was four adults. Two adult brothers and their parents.'

Ella shook her head. 'No. It's two single mums, each with one young kid. And I'm sure neither of them was called Hardman.'

'No. I spoke to one of the brothers myself. He sounded about our age or possibly a bit older and he said he wanted the cottage from Friday the 21st of December until Wednesday the 2nd of January for him, his younger brother and their parents. He told me that he and his brother would only be here from the 21st until Boxing Day but his parents would be here for the whole time. It's their Ruby Wedding anniversary and they actually met in this village over forty years ago.'

Ella shook her head again. 'Absolutely not. I spoke to someone called Cathy. She's booked the cottage for two weeks from this coming Wednesday, the 19th until Wednesday the 2nd, for her and her friend Christy. She said they each have a child and they want to give them an old-fashioned Christmas.'

'But the Hardmans have already booked it.' Mia shot an anxious look from Ella to Jet and back again.

'But so has Cathy whatshername. I told you about it last week. You never mentioned the Hardmans then.' Ella looked equally anxious. 'At least, I think I told you. I definitely wrote it on the pad beside the living room phone. I remember Gill and I were dashing out to the pub when the phone rang and you were at Jet's. I'm sure I told you the following day. Didn't I?'

Mia sighed and shook her head. 'No, Ella. You didn't.'

'Damn. I meant to.'

'You've got to stop writing things on that notepad and not telling me.'

'It's not my fault. If you made sure you looked at it every day, I wouldn't have to remember to tell you. We need to sort out some kind of system. Perhaps we should get one of those cork board things and hang it in the kitchen, near the kettle, and pin messages to it. That way we would both see it.'

'That's a good idea. But not a cork board. I don't like those things. Perhaps we could get one of those pretty blackboards I showed you in one of those online shops the other day. But how could I be sure you'd actually remember to write the message on it?'

'Excuse me,' Jet said, shaking his head. 'I think you've got something more important than a message board to sort out. It seems to me that you've got eight people arriving this week and they're all expecting to spend Christmas in Corner Cottage, which, if I remember correctly, only has four bedrooms. And even if it had more, I'm not sure either party would want to spend their holiday with another set of complete strangers.'

Mia blinked several times and stared from Jet to Ella, her mouth falling open as she did so.

'Oh. My. God. Jet's right! You're going to have to call your lot back and tell them there's been an error and they'll have to look for somewhere else.'

'Somewhere else? The woman told me she'd spent days on the internet looking for somewhere and everything she'd tried was booked. I can't tell her, her friend and their young kids that they'll have to spend Christmas at home. It'll break her heart. You didn't hear how excited she was. She would've gone on and on for hours if I hadn't told her I had to deal with an emergency.'

'What emergency?' Gill asked, furrowing his brows. 'I don't recall any emergencies last week.'

'I needed a glass of wine and we'd run out, remember?'

Mia tutted. 'Well, I can't tell the Hardmans. I told you. It's the parents' Ruby Wedding anniversary and they met here, in this village. Going somewhere else would ruin the whole thing for them.'

'Not as much as sharing a bathroom with someone you've never met,' Jet said, his mouth twitching at the corner.

Mia frowned at him. 'It's not funny, Jet, so as much as I love that grin of yours, be serious. We've got to find a solution to this.'

'The only solution,' Gill said, 'is to disappoint one set of people. You've only got one cottage to rent, and unless you're good at performing miracles, you can't make one cottage turn into two.'

'Oh hell.' Mia took a deep breath. 'It's my cottage so I suppose it'll have to be me who does it. And as I didn't take the booking from the woman, I can explain that it was an error. Perhaps if I offer her a free weekend sometime, it might let her down a bit more gently. I don't expect she'll be able to find somewhere else, but the sooner she knows, the better chance she'll have.' She sighed and walked towards the front door, glancing briefly at Jet who looked deep in thought.

'Er.' Ella looked apologetic. 'You may have a problem if you're thinking of telling my lot to look elsewhere. I don't believe I took a phone number, now I come to think about it.'

'What?' Mia stopped in her tracks. 'But they've paid the rental invoice, so you must have their email address at least.'

Ella cleared her throat. 'Um. No. I forgot to ask. As I said, I was in a rush.'

'If they haven't paid, how do we know they're coming?'

'Oh they're coming. I told you. The woman was over the moon about it. She'll obviously pay when she gets here on Wednesday.'

'Or she won't turn up,' Gill said. 'That'll solve your problem. Perhaps it would be wise to wait and see if she arrives, or if she calls back. She must've thought it was a bit odd not to have to pay in advance, or at least, leave a deposit.'

Mia frowned. 'But if she does turn up, I can't then tell her I've already rented it out to someone else and that she and her friend and their kids won't have anywhere to stay and will have to go home for Christmas, can I? And I can't let the Hardmans down. As I said, it's the parents' anniversary and they met in Little Pondale. And they have paid in advance.'

'Her number may still be in the call log on the phone,' Gill suggested.

'It was the landline,' Ella said.

Gill pulled a face and grinned. 'I know. I'm well aware you can't make or receive calls on mobiles. But all modern landline phones have a call log too. Unless you've deleted it. I don't think either of you would've done that.'

'That's good,' Mia said.

Ella nodded. 'Although it means you've got the awful task of telling the poor woman that she'll have to find somewhere else for her and her friend to give their kids an old-fashioned Christmas.'

Mia frowned. 'And whose fault is that?'

Ella shrugged and screwed up her face. 'Mine, I suppose. I really am sorry. Even more so for those poor kids.'

'Mia. Wait,' Jet said, as Mia continued towards the front door. 'There is another option.'

She turned to face him. 'Oh? What's that?'

He coughed lightly and adjusted the collar of his waterproof jacket as if it were too tight and then he looked her directly in the eyes. 'You could move in with me. Just for Christmas, I mean.'

Had Mia heard him correctly?

'Move in with you?'

He ran a hand through his lustrous, midnight-black hair and his mouth twitched. 'Don't look so shocked. It'll only be temporary. But it does solve your problem. That way, if the women and kids do arrive this Wednesday, you can rent them Corner Cottage, and then the Hardmans can have Sunbeam Cottage from this Friday and you can simply tell them that this cottage became available and is the nicer of the two. Which it definitely is. They'll be so pleased, they won't care that they're not getting the place they thought they were.'

'Move in with you for Christmas?' Mia still couldn't believe it. Jet had definitely come a long way in the last few months, but she hadn't expected this. He'd gone from a man who had never had a long-term relationship or told a woman he loved her; who only wanted fun and then waved women goodbye; who was so anti-relationships and marriage that it was almost unbelievable – to this. A man who was in a loving relationship with her. He told her he loved her every single day. Sometimes more than once a day. He'd shown her it was true. And now he was actually offering to let her move into Little Pond Farm … with him. Even if it was just for Christmas. Miracles clearly did happen. She looked him in the eyes. 'Are you sure, Jet?'

He frowned before the twitch at the corner of his mouth took hold again and burst into a loving smile. 'Absolutely. It'll only be for a couple of weeks and if we get the heavy snow the forecasters are predicting, it'll save either one of us from having to trudge through it to see each other.'

Ella coughed. 'Ahem. I hate to interrupt this astonishing moment, but what about me and Gill?'

'We could go back to my place in Cambridge for Christmas,' Gill suggested, but he didn't look keen.

'You're welcome to come and stay too,' Jet said, dragging his gaze from Mia and grinning at Ella. 'You know there're seven bedrooms in the farmhouse. But I'm not putting wooden reindeer or plastic snowmen, or anything else Christmas related on my roof, so don't even think about suggesting it.'

Ella grinned. 'Just the light-up candy canes down the length of your drive then and, of course, as your front lawn is much, much bigger than this one, possibly two or three snowmen, and maybe even two matching Christmas trees?'

'Too much?' Mia asked him, laughing, when she saw the look of horror on his face.

'Way too much. I'll agree to one tree, with lights, and that's it.'

'A big tree?' Mia coaxed. 'And maybe a row of candy canes leading to the door?'

He sighed as if he knew he'd lost the battle. 'Okay. One tree and one row of candy canes. But that's definitely it.' He smiled. 'So we're doing this? You're moving in to my farmhouse?'

Mia nodded. 'We'd love to. And I promise you Jet, this will be a Christmas you'll never forget.'

He gave a short burst of laughter as she ran to him and hugged and kissed him. 'I don't doubt that for a minute,' he said, bending his head to kiss her properly.

'We don't have time for that,' Ella interrupted. 'If we're moving in with you, we've got to start moving our stuff out of here.'

Mia eased herself out of the kiss and smiled. 'We don't have to move anything until Wednesday. If the women don't arrive, we can all stay put. And anyway, we haven't got much stuff to move. Most of it was Mattie's. It won't take long to shift our clothes and the few possessions I brought with me when I came to stay here. You still haven't moved any of your own stuff down, so it's just your clothes. Neither has Gill. But we will have to find a place for my rowing machine. We can't leave that in the dining room if the Hardmans have to have this cottage.'

Chapter Two

'Morning vicar.'

Glen Fox smiled at Ella and her friends, and returned the cheerful greeting. He had only been in Little Pondale for two weeks but was quickly getting to know the residents, most of whom, like Ella, Mia, Jet and Gill, seemed very friendly. But there was something a little odd in the way Ella looked at him and smiled; as if he reminded her of a private joke or some such thing.

'Your cottage is looking very festive,' Glen said, taking in the mass of lights, reindeer and snowmen occupying almost every square inch of the roof and front garden.

'You should see inside,' Ella replied, winking at him. 'And there's a tree, a couple of reindeer and another snowman in the back garden too. Mia and I love Christmas.'

Glen raised his brows. 'I would never have guessed. I hope that means I'll be seeing you all in church.'

'Ah.' Ella grinned at him. 'About that. We're not really church lovers since the last vicar tried to bump off Jet with one of the angels from the church roof, and got his girlfriend to send Mia threats.'

'And tampered with Jet's brakes,' Mia added.

Jet nodded. 'Not to mention embezzling church funds.'

'Yes,' Glen said, shaking his head. 'The Bishop filled me in regarding the church aspects, and I'm obliged to Hettie Turner for making me fully aware of the rest of the former Reverend Thomas Tyburn's nefarious activities. Disgraceful behaviour. We're all mortified. But I sincerely hope that one man's appalling dishonesty and criminal behaviour will not reflect on the rest of us. If there is anything I can do to persuade you that we're not all bad, I'll willingly do it.'

'You can reinstate the choir,' Mia said. 'Everyone in the village wants that. Choir practice was Tuesday evenings and we all miss it.'

Glen beamed at them. 'Then I have good news for you. Hettie was bending my ear ... I mean, Hettie was suggesting the very same thing in church this morning, and I've decided to do exactly that. Does that mean I can look forward to the pleasure of seeing you all in church this Tuesday evening?'

Mia and Ella grinned at one another.

'We'll all be there,' Mia said. 'You can count on it.'

'But I can't sing,' said Gill.

'That's never stopped Ella,' Jet joked.

'Oi! Watch it Jet Cross, or the vicar won't be the only one who tries to kill you,' Ella said, but she was laughing.

'Former vicar,' Glen corrected, smiling. 'Hettie also informed me that the choir has a carol singing evening for charity each year. Obviously it's rather short notice but I'm going to try to organise that for this coming Saturday. Her husband Fred has kindly offered to produce some leaflets. I'm off to see him now and they'll be dropping through all the letterboxes in the village today. May I put your names down for Saturday?'

'Of course,' Jet said. 'This will be Mia, Ella and Gill's first Christmas in Little Pondale, but I've been involved in the charity carol singing since I was old enough to walk and it's a really good event. Not only does it help the chosen charities, it's also fun for those taking part.' He directed his gaze to Mia. 'We carry candle lanterns and go from cottage to cottage, finally ending up at The Frog and Lily where Freda and Alec lay on a festive buffet, with turkey sandwiches, sausage rolls, mince pies, mulled wine and spiced hot cider punch. It usually turns into a bit of a party.'

Mia smiled. 'You don't have to convince me. I'm in.'

'You had me at The Frog and Lily.' Ella grinned at Jet and winked at Glen.

Gill frowned. 'Freda and Alec may not be feeling terribly festive this year. Didn't Toby say they might be going to Spain?'

'Yes he did,' Mia said. 'But he's not going. He told me that as much as he still loves his sister, he's not ready to forgive her and pretend that none of that stuff happened. He's going to stay and run the pub, even though that means it'll be the first Christmas his family has spent apart for as long as he can remember. Which is very sad, when you think about it.'

Jet nodded. 'True. But if I know Toby, and believe me, I do know Toby, he'll make sure it's Christmas as usual at The Frog and Lily.'

'Well,' Glen said. 'That's something else for us all to look forward to. I'll put you on the list for Saturday. I'd better get to Fred and Hettie's now or Hettie will send out a search party. See you all on Tuesday. Have a lovely Sunday.'

'Er, vicar,' Ella called after him as he turned and walked away. 'You're heading in the wrong direction. Duckdown Cottage is two doors down the lane, not across the village green.'

Glen glanced over his shoulder and smiled. The sarcasm in Ella's voice was evident.

'Thank you, Ella. I know it is. I simply thought I'd pop into Lake's Bakes and see if Jenny had some of those delicious mini panettones. She very kindly gave me a gift box of baked treats as a welcome present, and while everything in the box was delicious to say the least, the mini panettone made me feel as if I'd died and gone to heaven.'

'The cinnamon swirls are pretty heavenly too,' Mia said.

Ella grinned. 'All Jenny's buns are divine, aren't they, vicar?'

Glen was once again certain there was something in the way Ella winked at him, but he simply nodded, smiled, waved and walked on. Ella was right though; Jenny Lake's buns were indeed divine. And Jenny was rather special too.

He hadn't been particularly keen to take over at St Michael and All Angels, especially after hearing what went on there, and the thought of living in a village appealed to him about as much as going on a day trip to hell, but his uncle was the Bishop and had asked him for a favour. Glen couldn't turn him down. Besides, it was only a temporary post. Someone would replace him in the New Year, or the diocese might even merge two parishes into one, so his uncle said. In any event, he merely had to spend a few weeks here, and that couldn't be too bad. Dull and boring maybe, but he had books to read and the scenery was stunning. He had planned to try his hand at watercolour painting; that was something his mother loved to do and he had always promised himself that, when he had some spare time on his hands, he would give it a go himself. And then, at exactly seven on the first night he arrived, his doorbell rang and when he had opened the door to his cottage, he thought his dreams had come true. The most beautiful woman he had ever seen was standing on his doorstep, her wild, red hair like dancing flames in the bitterly cold north-east wind and the light from the street lamps; her cherry-red lips the epitome of the word 'temptation'; her warm hazel eyes like beacons of hope in the dull and boring weeks ahead. He had actually been lost for words.

And so, it seemed, had she. But she was the first to speak.

'I brought you these,' she had said, smiling up at him with outstretched hands. 'I'm Jenny Lake from Lake's Bakes, the bakery across the village green.' She nodded in that general direction. 'I'm fairly new to the village too. I've taken over from my cousin, Justin Lake who owns the place. He moved to Hollywood and he's already a star even though his film's not out until next year. I've come here from Florence. I loved it there but … well, sadly my boyfriend broke my heart and I needed to get away, so it was perfect timing.' She stopped suddenly, winced, screwed up her face and blushed profusely. 'Sorry. I have no idea why I told you all that. I don't usually tell complete strangers my entire life story.' Her colour deepened and she averted her gaze. 'Here. I've brought you a selection of my cakes and biscuits. Just a few to have with a mug of cocoa tonight before you go to bed, or with coffee for breakfast, or … Oh gosh. Sorry. My mind seems to be wandering. Um.

Lovely to meet you, Reverend. Welcome to Little Pondale. Good night.'

She had turned and hurried away, the wind playing with that incredible red hair and all he could think of to say was, 'Thanks.'

He shook his head and smiled now as he crunched his way across the grass, the remnants of the morning frost still glistening in the pale lemon sunlight. She must've thought he was a complete imbecile that night. And her opinion of him clearly hadn't improved much since.

He'd gone to the bakery the following morning to thank her properly but she had seemed a little off with him and the bakery had been packed. That was a surprise. Little Pondale was hardly large, by any stretch of the imagination but every single villager and their relatives must have been in the bakery that day. And every day since. People were actually coming now from other villages, some from miles around and some from the nearest town, fifteen miles away. Who could blame them? Jenny's cakes were the best he had ever tasted and her bread was like no other bread he'd eaten. Everything she made was delicious. And he would know. He'd bought something each day for the last two weeks. At this rate, he would have the girth of Father Christmas if he wasn't careful.

But he still hadn't managed to say more than two or three words to her. It was true that he wasn't known for giving lengthy sermons, but he could usually have a long conversation with people. Not with Jenny Lake, apparently. All the while he was in the queue, he could think of lots of clever things to say. Lots of compliments to pay her. Even a few jokes to make her smile. But the minute she looked into his eyes and said those fateful words, 'Hello Reverend. What can I tempt you with today?' he turned into a gibbering idiot. Once, he was sure, he actually dribbled. Or perhaps it just felt as if he had. In any event, all he ever seemed to manage was to point at something on display, hand over some cash, smile like a clown on cocaine, mumble an inaudible, 'Thanks', and stumble out of the bakery.

This time it would be different. Today would be the day he finally had a conversation with Jenny Lake. A sensible conversation. And, if he was really brave, he might even ask her if she would join the choir. He was sure she would have the voice of an angel.

Chapter Three

Jenny Lake was about to close up. She had been on her feet since five and opened the bakery at seven. Being a small shop in a village meant she wasn't governed by the Sunday opening hour restrictions of stores and supermarkets, but she always closed at twelve on Sundays. Working six and a half days a week took its toll and she relished her lazy Sunday afternoons. Not that she did much lazing. She took the opportunity to get out and about; to walk along the glorious, sandy beach behind the cottages on Lily Pond Lane, or to the top of Frog Hill where the view was three and sixty degrees of sea, and countryside and a sky that seemed to go on forever. Her cousin Justin had left her his car, so sometimes she went for a drive to one of the neighbouring villages, or into the nearest town to browse around the shops. But no matter where she went or what she did, her mind, and more particularly, her heart, were never far away from

Florence. She'd definitely left her heart in Florence, but for all the wrong reasons. There were no doubt shards of it, like broken marble, scattered around for everyone to see and point at as they visited the galleries and museums. "Wasn't that Jenny Lake's heart?" they would say. "The one that Silvio Meoni sculpted to love and trust and believe in him before he smashed it to smithereens with his lies and deceit and cheating."

Jenny clicked the lock on the door and was just about to draw down the blind when she saw Reverend Glen Fox striding towards the bakery. She glanced at her watch. It was precisely twelve. She could tell him she was closed and send him away, but the smile on his face when he saw her was so warm, so genuine, that she didn't have it in her to do that. Besides, it wouldn't take her more than thirty seconds to serve him. He hardly ever said more than one word to her. Even the night she'd taken that welcome box to his cottage all he'd said was, 'Thanks'. It seemed very odd for a vicar. More so since she'd attended one of his services. He hadn't seen her as she'd crept in and sat at the very back but he had been eloquent on that occasion and his sermon had been friendly and inspirational. He'd been confident; he'd smiled a lot, he'd even made a few small jokes, all in good taste. He'd been the complete opposite of the man he was whenever he stood in front of her. The only consistent things about him were that he was tall, broad-shouldered, had the sort of blond hair that made you want to run your fingers through it and the type of mouth that made you want to kiss it. But it was his eyes that had taken her breath away that first night. Blue eyes that reminded her of a summer day in Florence – eyes that twinkled with a hint of devilment. Not at all the kind of eyes one expected to see on a vicar's face, however handsome he may be. Although why couldn't vicars be sexy? They were human, after all. Not that she was in the least bit interested in him in that way. Without her heart, she couldn't ever fall in love again. And that was just the way she wanted it. Love was for fools, for dreamers, for those who had no idea of reality. Or for one or two lucky ones, such as Mia and Jet, and Ella and Gill. Perhaps one day when she was old, like Hettie, she might love again. She might find the happiness that Hettie had with Fred. But for now, she would get out of bed each day, look at the grey English skies or the odd day of pale sunshine, like today, and wonder what Silvio was doing beneath the ever-blue skies of Florence. And which woman he was with today.

She sighed, unlocked the door and opened it before walking back behind the counter.

'Hello Reverend. What can I tempt you with today?'

To her astonishment, he actually replied, although it did seem to take forever and his gaze darted around the bakery for a good few seconds before he took a deep breath and finally looked her in the eyes.

'Hello, Jenny. I'm rather hoping I can tempt you.'

And for one brief moment, the way he smiled at her and the way his blue eyes twinkled, she thought there was a very slight chance he could.

'Oh?' she managed, sounding more like him than he did.

'I'm reinstating the choir,' he said. 'From this Tuesday evening. And on Saturday we're going carol singing around the village for charity. Mia and Jet and Ella and Gill have said yes and I'm hoping you will too. It should be fun and it is for a good cause. Please say you will. We'll finish in the pub and we may even have a buffet there, but if not, I'll organise something in the church hall. Will you come with me? With us, I mean.' He gave a little cough and a slight frown as if he was displeased with what he'd said. 'Unless you already have plans, of course. I realise it's short notice and it's a Saturday and a girl like you probably has a date or something.'

'A girl like me? What does that mean, Reverend?'

He turned the colour of one of her raspberry cheesecakes. 'Oh! Um. A girl as beautiful as you, I mean. Um. You're young, you're attractive, you're single. You are single, aren't you?'

She glared at him. 'Yes, Reverend. And I plan to stay that way.'

'I'm so sorry. I didn't mean to offend you.' He looked genuinely concerned.

She gave him a small smile. 'I didn't mean to snap. Sore subject. But as for the rest of it, I'm not sure you'd want me either in your choir or at the carol singing. I've got the kind of voice that makes a dog sound like a prima donna. Believe me, no one wants to hear me sing. Although I could make you a fortune if people had to pay to get me to stop.'

He smiled and his eyes held a warmth that made her feel as if she were sitting in front of a cosy fire. 'I'm sure that's not true.'

She laughed and nodded. 'It is, Reverend. Believe me. I rarely lie.'

'Well, you could come along anyway, couldn't you? Just to join in with the festive spirit.'

'To be honest, I'm not feeling very festive. Christmas was never my favourite time of year and this year I … Well, that doesn't matter. Let's just say I'm feeling even less festive than usual. You really don't want me around.'

'I do want you, Jenny.' He said it so quickly and firmly that it seemed to surprise him as much as it did her. 'I do want you to join us, that is. We all do. Most of the village will be there, I'm sure of it.'

She met his eyes before turning away. 'Okay. I'll think about it. I was just closing up so unless there's anything else, I'll wish you a good Sunday afternoon, Reverend.'

'Actually, there is. Firstly, I'd really like it if you'd call me Glen instead of Reverend. Reverend makes me feel old and unapproachable somehow. Secondly, I'd like three of those, please. I'm going to see Hettie and Fred and I'm already late so one of your delicious treats may soften the glare dear Hettie will no doubt give me. What are they?'

Jenny smiled enthusiastically. She was always happy to talk about the things she baked.

'Cavallucci. They're a type of biscotti made with flour, candied fruit, anise, coriander, and mine have walnuts and almonds in. They usually only have one or the other but why have one variety of nut when you can have two? Would you like to taste one first in case you don't like it?'

He shook his head and smiled. 'No need. I've loved everything I've had so far and I'm sure these, cavallucci, did you say?' She nodded and he continued: 'I'm certain they'll be equally delicious.'

Jenny beamed at him. 'I think you're my biggest fan, Reverend.'

'You have no idea. And it's Glen, remember?'

The way he said that made her meet his eyes and although she hadn't meant to, she gave a little sigh. She quickly turned away and grabbed a paper bag and some tongs. She picked up three cavallucci and slipped them in the bag, twisting the corners as she handed it to him.

'Enjoy,' she said, avoiding his stare. 'And as I've already cashed up, they're my treat.' She hadn't cashed up, but he wouldn't know that.

'That's very kind. But I still haven't thanked you properly for that gift box you gave me the night I arrived. For some reason, I always end up sounding like an idiot whenever I come here. And I may as well do so again. Let me cook dinner for you one night this week. I'm a pretty good cook. Although not in your league, obviously.'

His smile lit up his entire face. A handsome, trustworthy face. But she'd been duped by good looks before. She wouldn't fall for that a second time.

'No,' she said, rather more abruptly than she meant to. 'I mean. No thank you. That's kind, Reverend, but I only gave you that welcome gift because you were the new vicar. I'm not looking for a relationship, or a date, or anything of that sort, thanks.'

'Sorry,' he said, a touch of sadness in his tone. 'What about a friend? I believe I can be a good one of those.' He gave an optimistic smile.

She didn't know what to say and he obviously took her silence as a rejection.

'And, I've done it again. Behaved like a complete idiot. I apologise. I'll leave you to enjoy your afternoon. But if you ever do need a friend, Jenny, I'm just across the green. Thanks for the cavallucci.'

He marched off before she had a chance to reply, and as she watched him go, the sun disappeared behind a bank of cloud and tiny flakes of white fluttered from the sky.

Snow.

That was all she needed.

She hated snow almost as much as she hated Christmas … and possibly even, men.

Chapter Four

'It's snowing!' Mia tipped back her head and closed her eyes, allowing snowflakes to land on her face.

'Wonderful,' Jet said, but he didn't sound particularly enthusiastic. 'Perhaps you could decide where on this roof you want the snowman, so that Gill and I can come down.'

'Where's your Christmas spirit?' Ella asked, grinning up at him as she linked arms with Mia on the front lawn of Corner Cottage.

Jet pulled a face. 'I left it on the roof of Sunbeam Cottage. I didn't think we were going to put anything on this roof other than a string of lights.'

'We weren't,' Mia replied, opening her eyes and smiling up at him. 'But as Ella said, if we do rent this cottage to the women and their kids, we've got to have a snowman or two. Put it on the right side of the chimney. We'll put the other snowman on the left side of the lawn and then you and Gill can put a row of the light-up candy canes along the front edge, and we'll fix the wreath to the door.'

'We'll do that,' Gill offered. 'I've seen you and Ella with a hammer and nails and it's not a pretty sight.'

Jet nodded. 'Leave this to us. You go to Hettie's and find out exactly what she wants to do for her place. Then, unless you plan to volunteer our services to anyone else in the village, perhaps we can spend the rest of the afternoon indoors, in the warm, roasting chestnuts on the fire and drinking hot, spiced cider.'

Mia laughed. 'Roasting chestnuts? I think I've made you watch too many Christmas movies over the last two weeks. And for a farmer and a rugby player, you're a bit of a wimp when it comes to cold weather. Plus, I didn't volunteer your services. You were the one who said you didn't want Fred climbing up any ladders at his age, and certainly not in this weather. You were also the one who said, before we left your house this morning, that you'd probably end up putting up other people's decorations, so it was best to leave Little M at home because you didn't want her chasing strings of fairy lights across the lawns.' They had recently changed the name of Jet's rescued dog, from Mattie to Little M because it was getting confusing. Whenever they mentioned Mia's great-aunt Mattie, the excitable little crossbreed would come racing up and bounce around like a wind-up toy. Although in fact, the change of name hadn't stopped her doing that.

Jet grinned. 'That's true. But I do like roasted chestnuts. And Hettie makes a mean, spiced cider. She did say she'd have a batch of it ready for us this afternoon.'

'She's probably stirring her cauldron right now,' Ella joked. 'Not that I'd say that in front of her. Come on, Mia. Let's leave them to it. I quite like the sound of hot, spiced cider. Perhaps we can see how she makes it, and if she gives us the recipe, Gill can make some more for us.'

'I heard that,' Gill said, as Mia and Ella turned to walk away. 'Why can't you and Mia have a go at making it?'

Ella glanced over her shoulder and laughed. 'Don't be ridiculous, Gill. You know full well that Mia and I are even worse at cooking than we are at D.I.Y.'

Mia grinned at her. 'But I can make mulled wine. This cider thing can't be much different. All we probably need to do is chuck a few bottles of cider in a pot, add some spices and let it simmer. We can do that.'

They walked down the path of Corner Cottage and turned up Lily Pond Lane towards Hettie and Fred's. Hettie had waved at them as they had walked past earlier and said how much she liked the decorations they'd been putting up at Sunbeam Cottage.

'Fred's going to put a few up here this afternoon, my dears' she'd said, clasping her hands beneath her ample bosom. 'But we're waiting for the vicar. Fred's making some leaflets for him about the charity carol singing this Saturday. I'm sure you'll all be coming to that. I do like this new vicar but his time-keeping needs some attention. Said he'd be here at twelve and it's ten minutes past already.'

'He's just nipped over to the bakery,' Jet had told her. 'We saw him a couple of minutes ago. We're off to put some decorations up at Corner Cottage, but it won't take long, I hope.' He had glanced at Mia and grinned. 'Don't let Fred go climbing any ladders, Hettie. Gill and I will pop round when we've finished down the lane and we'll put up anything you want.'

'That's kind of you, deary. I'll tell you what. I'm making some of my special cider. The hot, spiced one you've always liked. I'll make an extra batch for all of you, my dears. Nipped to the bakery, you say? Hmm. I've seen him there quite a lot these last two weeks. Since the morning after he arrived, in fact, my dears. Either our new vicar has a sweet tooth, or he's sweet on something else, if you get my drift. Not that I'm one to gossip these days, as you know. But Jenny Lake's a pretty little thing, isn't she? And those hazel eyes of hers. So sad-looking. I was only saying to my dear Fred the other day that I'm sure that girl's got a broken heart. I know the signs. But then so do you, don't you deary?' She gave Mia a little smile. 'But look at you now. Head over heels in love with our Jet. And he's head over heels in love with you. And, as you know, that's something no one in this village ever thought we'd see. But here I go, talking ten chickens at a time. Better let you get on or it'll be dark before you know it. I don't like these dark nights. Apart from cuddling up on the sofa with my dear Fred, and Prince Gustav. Which reminds me. I forgot to ask the vicar if he likes rats. Perhaps I'd better put dear Prince Gustav back in his cage, just in case. If the vicar ever turns up that is, my dears.'

They'd finally managed to get away but Hettie's words had given Mia food for thought and now that she and Ella were alone, she brought the subject up.

'Do you think Hettie was right about Jenny?'

Ella glanced at her. 'About her having a broken heart? Possibly. When I first met her, back in November shortly arrived she arrived, I said that she must've had her pick of hunky, gorgeous, hot-blooded Italian men, and asked why on earth she left. She looked as if she'd seen a ghost. So I added, 'or beautiful women' because you never know, do you? And she smirked at that and said something like, "No. It's men. Or it was. I'm not interested in any of that now." I asked why not and she simply said she had the bakery to run. I've tried to ask her personal stuff like that since then but she's always very cagey. She'll go on for hours about what's in her cakes but ask about her personal life and she shuts her mouth tighter than an oven door.'

Mia nodded. 'I've noticed that. A couple of times I've asked about life in Florence. She's told me about the galleries and museums, about the cafes and restaurants, about the smells from the shops and the colours of the sky and surrounding countryside. But the minute I ask how she spent her time and if there was anyone special, she clams up. I've asked her round for dinner a few times, too, and she's always got some excuse, like orders to place, or the books to do, or a recipe she needs to get right. She's polite and says, things like, "Thanks. Perhaps another time." I've given up asking now. It's as if she wants to be left alone.'

'So if the vicar is interested, he doesn't stand much chance, does he?'

'I don't think so. But then again, as you said, you never know. And look at me and Jet. When I arrived here, no one would've thought for one minute that Jet and I would be together. But we are.'

'Except Mattie, who planned the whole thing,' Ella reminded her.

Not that Mia needed reminding. She had a great deal to thank her great-aunt Matilda for – in addition to the money and property she'd been left. If Mattie hadn't put that condition in her will which meant Mia had to come and live in Little Pondale to inherit Sunbeam Cottage, Jet and her may never have met. Mia possibly might have visited the cottage briefly to see what it was like but then she probably would've simply sold it and bought somewhere in London with the money. When she'd been told about the will and about the great-aunt she didn't know she had, leaving London to live in a tiny village wouldn't even have crossed her mind. She had only done so because she had to. Having been fired from her accountancy admin job, and been struggling with her rent, the chance to live rent-free in a cottage and have some cash to play with, was a gift from the gods. Well, a gift from her great-aunt. Now, she couldn't bear the thought of ever leaving. Not that she would. She intended to spend her life here, with Jet. And that was another little miracle. The fact that he'd now said she could move in with him. Even if it was just for Christmas.

Mia smiled and nodded. 'Yes. But look how much he's changed. Did you ever think you'd hear him suggest I move in with him? At least, so soon? Albeit temporarily.'

Ella shook her head. 'Nope. That was a complete surprise. But if I'm not mistaken, you have me to thank for that.'

Mia raised her brows. 'Really? How?'

Ella grinned. 'Because if I hadn't taken that other booking, and then forgot to tell you, the cottage wouldn't have been double-booked and you wouldn't need to rent out your own cottage, so Jet wouldn't need to have made the offer.'

'That's true.' Mia laughed and nudged Ella's arm. 'For once, your complete incompetence has done us both a favour.'

'Oi! I'm not completely incompetent. I'm a talented editor, a fabulous best friend, a wonderful sister and, according to Gill, a sex goddess.'

'Okay. Those are all true. And speaking of being a wonderful sister, do you have any more news about when the baby is due?'

'No. Garrick still says it's January but Fiona was huge when I saw them at Mum and Dad's last month and even Gill said he wonders if they've got the timing right. Not that we want to think about that, do we?'

'It's okay, Ella. I'm completely fine with it now. I love Jet more than I thought it was possible to love anyone and I could even chat with Garrick now, like we used to, and not feel the slightest pang of sadness or regret.'

'He'll be pleased to hear that. He always asks after you, every time we speak. Even Fiona sent her love when we chatted this morning. Now that you're so happy with Jet, she likes you again, I think. Oh, but I forgot to tell you that, too. We definitely must get some sort of message board and stick it in the kitchen.'

'What were you saying about not being incompetent?' Mia teased. 'Gosh. It's getting colder and these snowflakes are getting bigger by the second. Come on. Let's get to Hettie's and get warm.' She glanced back down the lane and laughed. 'Poor Jet and Gill. They'll be frozen to death by the time they've finished.'

'Yes. But we can warm them up later. If you get my drift, as Hettie would say.'

'God, Ella. Don't get me thinking about sex when we've got to spend at least an hour with Hettie. You know the woman can virtually read my mind these days. She seems to know when I'm thinking about it.'

'That's because you're always thinking about it. You and Jet can't seem to keep your hands off each other. And I suppose it isn't really such a big deal that he's suggested you move in for Christmas. You spend almost all your time together anyway. Either you're at his place or he's at yours. Since Halloween, I don't think you two have spent one night apart, have you?'

Mia considered it and shook her head. 'No. I don't think we have. We sometimes say we will, and we really plan to, but somehow, either he turns up at mine, or I find myself at his front door. It's weird.'

Ella chuckled. 'It's not. You're simply madly in love. And we're the same, I suppose, so I can hardly talk. Gill and I haven't spent a night apart either. Love's a very funny thing.'

'Love's wonderful. I think everyone should be in love. Hmm. I wonder if Hettie is right about the vicar liking Jenny? And I wonder if there's anything we can do to get the two of them together? Glen Fox is rather gorgeous and Jenny does seem sad.'

'But his stay here is only temporary, and we've got a novel to write, remember? You, me and Gill are supposed to be spending all our free time on that. We don't have time to plot and scheme to get Jenny and Glen together, especially as we have no idea if they even like one another. And if you're going to be renting out two cottages now, we've got to keep both of them clean and tidy. We can't ask Hettie to do it all, can we?'

Mia sighed. 'I suppose you're right.'

'Mia?' Ella gave her a questioning look as they reached Hettie's front door. 'You're going to try to do it, aren't you? You're going to try to get Jenny and gorgeous Glen together.'

Mia grinned. 'Well, it is Christmas, after all. Everyone should be in love at Christmas.'

Ella tutted before throwing Mia a cheeky grin. 'Well I suppose that'll add a whole new meaning to my vicar and tart jokes, won't it? Jenny does bake a rather scrumptious Sicilian lemon tart.'

Chapter Five

Glen Fox opened his bedroom curtains and frowned. From the moment he had woken up he had told himself the sun would be shining and the snow from yesterday would have melted, but as soon as he rolled over and glanced towards the window it had been obvious that Monday was not going to be a sunny day. No soft yellow beams of light filtered through the tiny gap between the curtains and the window. Instead, the room seemed grey and somewhat cold, even though he knew the heating was on full blast. Glen didn't like the cold. Still, as he padded towards the window, he hoped; but there it was, blanketing the lane and the village green, covering the thatched roofs, and hiding the ice on the frozen pond.

Snow.

At least an inch of it. Possibly even two.

It had snowed on and off all yesterday afternoon and at one point, when he was helping

Jet and Gill put up Christmas decorations on Hettie and Fred's cottage, it had snowed so hard they had to stop and go inside until it eased off.

Eating several of Hettie's cranberry and orange, mince pies and drinking two mugs of her hot, spiced cider may not have been a good idea, especially after he'd already eaten one of the cavallucci he'd bought from Lake's Bakes, but he was very glad he, Jet and Gill had already finished decorating the roof and didn't have to go back up the ladder. That cider was lethal. He needed to bear that in mind for future visits to Hettie's.

Then for one brief hour after they had finished the decorations and gone their separate ways, the sun had come back out and some of the snow melted, as he had tried to walk off the effects of Hettie's cider. But more fell in the evening as he walked across the lane from his cottage to the church, and obviously more had fallen overnight.

It looked pretty enough, but it made it difficult for many people to get about, especially the elderly and the infirm. He'd have to ask around and see if there were any villagers who may need help. Having only been in Little Pondale for two weeks, he still hadn't got around to meeting all the villagers, even though the place was tiny. More than once, when he rang a bell or knocked on a door, he wondered if the residents were inside and merely avoiding him, or whether they were indeed 'out' each time he had called to introduce himself.

Attendance at his services was acceptable for a village of this size, but at least one third of the population hadn't set foot inside St Michael and All Angels since he'd taken over and some of those who had, had only gone once or twice to get a look at him, he was sure. Hettie had informed him that the turnout for him was better than for the previous incumbent, which didn't say much for religion in Little Pondale.

It wasn't his problem though. All he had to do was get through Christmas and the New Year and he'd be out of here by the end of January, if not sooner, according to his uncle, the Bishop.

The trouble was, it was his problem. He loved his job and he firmly believed all communities needed a place to go for spiritual guidance, or for comfort, or merely for a listening ear. He had a very modern view of religion. Some people might call it odd. He wanted the congregation to go to church, whether or not they believed in God. He wanted them to feel welcome, to feel a part of something bigger. From there, they might find God, or they might not. It was his job to show them the path and lead the way. He certainly wasn't going to force them to stay on it.

He glanced across the village green towards Lake's Bakes. From his cottage he could see the driveway, the front step leading to Baker's Cottage and the bakery at the side, which had many years ago, no doubt, been a stable or a barn. It had only been a bakery since Justin Lake's great-great-grandfather had bought the cottage in 1899, or so Hettie had told him.

He wondered if he should go back there after his ridiculous behaviour yesterday. What was he? Nine years old? He'd virtually begged Jenny for her friendship. He tutted at his own stupidity. He had sounded pathetic, sad and lonely. What on earth must she have thought? No wonder she hadn't replied.

But if he didn't go back, wouldn't that make things worse? Surely his best bet was to behave as if yesterday had meant nothing. That his comment was simply an ordinary, everyday remark and not one that he should feel mortified about.

And he really liked the cavallucci. He also liked mince pies. Did Jenny bake mince pies? He could say he'd had some at Hettie's and they had given him a craving for more. Yes. That sounded reasonable.

And there was no time like the present.

Chapter Six

Mia had a plan. She'd spent all Sunday evening thinking about it. Well, not quite all of the evening. During dinner, she, Ella and Gill, with Jet's additional input, had chatted over a few more ideas for the next chapters of the novel they were writing. Not that it was getting very far, what with Ella having more and more editing work recently. Gill was also working on his book about his grandfather, Guillaume De Fonteneau and the French Resistance during World War II and the part Mia's great-aunt also played. The truth was, Mia had enjoyed the months she'd spent unravelling Mattie's past, and now that she had read and re-read Mattie's diaries, she sometimes felt a little lacking and inadequate. As if she, herself, should have some sort of mission or dynamic purpose to her life, instead of merely bobbing along happily from day to day. Ella had her job as a freelance editor; Gill was a freelance journalist when he wasn't working on one of his books. But since losing her boring job in London and moving to Little Pondale, Mia hadn't had an occupation. Not that she needed one. She was rich now, thanks to Mattie, and she would never have to work again. But she needed to do something after reading about Mattie's own life, and writing the novel was supposed to be her occupation now. The problem was, the fiction didn't seem nearly as exciting as the facts of Mattie's life and to tell the truth, Mia's heart wasn't in it. When she'd mentioned this to Jet, he'd understood, but he said that only she could decide what she wanted her future to look like and as long as he was in it, he was happy to discuss it anytime, and would support her no matter what she chose to do.

And right now, she had chosen to be a matchmaker.

Okay, it was hardly earth-shattering, but helping people find happiness was a noble and admirable task. That's what she told herself in any event. She didn't mention it to Jet though. Not because she thought he wouldn't approve. Although there was a possibility he might not. But because she thought he might say something to Glen, and she couldn't have that. If Glen knew she was intending to set him up with Jenny, he might very well refuse to cooperate. Men were stubborn like that. Jet was a prime example. If he hadn't been so stubborn, he and Mia would've been together weeks earlier than Halloween.

No. The fewer people who knew of her plan, the better. She'd probably tell Ella though.

'Right,' Jet said, kissing her on the cheek as she sat at the kitchen table in Sunbeam Cottage, cradling her second mug of coffee and thinking through her plan as Little M lay curled up in her basket beside the Range. 'I'm off to do farm stuff. What've you got planned for the day?'

'Oh, nothing much.' Mia put her mug on the table, stood up and slid her arms around his waist. 'I know we won't be sure if we're going to come and stay with you until the first lot of guests turn up on Wednesday but I was thinking that your farmhouse needs some decorations anyway. Especially if we're going to have Christmas dinner there. And we are going to do that, aren't we? No matter what?'

He pulled her closer and grinned. 'Yes. We agreed it makes sense. My place is larger than this and the dining table can easily accommodate sixteen. Not that we're going to have sixteen people, are we?'

Mia ran a finger across the light stubble on his chin. 'You need a shave.'

'Which is another bonus of you spending Christmas at mine. I don't have to remember to bring my razor to come and stay here the night.'

'Or I could buy you one to keep here. I'm rich now, after all. We could have two of everything. One lot for here, one lot for your place.' Why had she said that? She wanted to spend Christmas at his farmhouse. Ever since he'd suggested it as an option yesterday she'd been praying that both lot of bookings turned up so that she, Ella and Gill would have to move into Little Pond Farm for the holidays.

'We could,' he said. 'I'd quite like two of you. One that I could take with me and have beside me all day, and one that could do whatever she wanted to do with her day.'

Mia laughed. 'Nice sentiment, but saying that out loud sounded a bit creepy.'

Jet laughed too. 'It did, didn't it? So how many people are we having for Christmas dinner? And what sort of decorations are you thinking the farmhouse needs? Please don't let Ella say those plastic snowmen or the twig reindeer because as much as I love you, I'm not having those inside my home.'

'Noted. No snowmen or reindeer indoors. Including Hettie and Fred, we're having eight for dinner. But I was wondering if we shouldn't also invite Jenny because otherwise she'll be on her own. And also, Glen, because so will he. But I was thinking that we ought to have a little test run first. Just in case they don't get on or something.'

Jet gave her a curious look. 'Why wouldn't they get on?'

Mia shrugged. 'Oh I don't know. Sometimes people simply don't. And although Hettie seems to prefer Glen to Tom, she may not be able to be polite to him all day. You know Hettie. A test run beforehand would mean Christmas Day wouldn't be ruined by people falling out.'

'Would it?' He grinned and kissed her on the nose, his blue eyes glinting with merriment. 'Why do I get the feeling there's something you're not telling me?'

Mia tried to look shocked. 'I have no idea. You know I tell you everything.'

He laughed at that. 'Yeah, right. So when were you thinking of having this trial run? And are you going to come and start decorating today?'

'Well. Tuesday is choir practice. Wednesday, the first lot of guests should be arriving. Thursday is your rugby training. Friday, the other guests arrive. Saturday is the charity carol evening, and Sunday is the twenty-third, which is far too close to Christmas if anything goes wrong. So that only leaves tonight, really.'

'Tonight? You want to hold a fake Christmas dinner tonight? At my place?'

'No, of course not. I'd like to have a little supper party tonight at your place. I'll ask Hettie to make her hot, spiced cider and some of those delicious cranberry and orange mince pies we had yesterday, and Jenny to bring some cakes, and Gill can make a turkey Thai curry, or something. And we can all put up the decorations. There's nothing quite as good to get everyone in the festive spirit as putting up decorations.'

'Yes. I noticed that yesterday when my fingers were dropping off from the cold. Gill and I both said how incredibly festive we were feeling.' He gave her a devilish grin and squeezed her tight.

She matched his grin and kissed him on the chin. 'You should've worn gloves. Wear them tonight when you, Gill and Glen are doing the outside decorations. Now go and water those cows, or whatever it is you do. I've got a list to write.'

He raised his brows. 'Hold on. Me, Gill and Glen? Do they know how they're going to be spending this evening?'

'Not yet. I'll tell Gill as soon as he gets up and I'll pop over to the vicarage at nine. Probably not polite to go before then. Not that a vicar has normal business hours, does he?'

'And what if one, or both of them don't want to go along with your plans?'

She looked at him in disbelief. 'Why wouldn't they? It's Christmas.'

He shook his head but he was chuckling to himself. 'They might have their own plans for tonight.'

'It's Monday and this is Little Pondale. What plans could anyone have that couldn't be changed? So you're okay with it? Shall I tell everyone to be at the farmhouse by six-thirty?'

He nodded and kissed her goodbye. 'I'm okay with it. But I still get the feeling there's something you're not telling me. Ah. Morning, Gill. My beautiful girlfriend has planned your entire day. Have a good one. See you later.' He winked at Mia, slapped Gill playfully on the shoulder and marched along the hall to the front door, with Little M at his heels.

Gill yawned and scratched his head. 'What was that? I missed it. I think I had too much of Hettie's cider yesterday, and then that wine with dinner. Or perhaps it was the brandy afterwards. Anyway, I feel like I've been dragged down a rabbit hole and used as a bed.'

'That doesn't make any sense at all,' Mia said, grinning as she poured him coffee. She shoved the mug in front of him as he collapsed on a chair and slumped across the table. 'And you need to sober up pretty quickly. We've got a lot to do today. I was hoping you'd go to the shops but clearly Ella and I will have to do that. I need you to make a turkey Thai curry or something equally delicious for supper tonight. We're putting up the decorations at Jet's and we're having a few people over to help. Are you up for that?'

He raised bloodshot eyes to her face and after a second or two, he nodded. 'Curry. Supper. Decorations. Jet. Got it. Thanks for the coffee.'

Ella positively bounced into the kitchen. 'Morning all! God, Gill. You look rough. Did you fall out of bed while I was in the shower? I thought I heard a thump but when I came out of the bathroom, there was no sign of you.'

He nodded. 'I think so.'

Mia bit back her laugh and glanced at Ella. 'I'm glad you're dressed and ready. We need to go shopping for food and more decorations. We're going to have a little supper party at Jet's tonight. I know he said yesterday that he's got decorations but he's a man, so we all know what they'll be like. We definitely need some new ones to add to the ones he's got.'

'Ooh, Christmas shopping!' Ella gleefully replied. 'I'm up for that. And a supper party sounds good. But why tonight?'

'I don't have time to explain.' Mia poured Ella a coffee before grabbing her handbag. 'I'll tell you later. I'm off to Jenny's then to the vicar's cottage. I'll be back in about half an hour. Do you think you can get Gill to tell you what he needs to make the turkey Thai curry and anything else he fancies making, and write a list? We'll go to the shops as soon as I get back. Is that okay?'

'Yep.' Ella grabbed a pen and pad from a drawer as Mia dashed towards the hall.

'This is going to be such fun, Ella. I just know it is.'

Chapter Seven

Jenny stared out at the sheet of white outside the bakery and wondered, yet again why she hadn't been brave enough to stay in Florence. But she knew why. Silvio's family owned the pasticceria where she had worked for the last two years. She couldn't stay there once she discovered his betrayal. Neither could she remain in her apartment because that came with the job. When Justin had called and told her he was leaving Little Pondale and would have to close the bakery, it had felt as if it was meant to be. The timing couldn't have been better. And she had been the one to suggest that she come and take over while he was away.

'It's over with me and Silvio,' she'd told him. 'I could do with a change of scene. Why don't I come and take over the bakery for you and, if it's okay with you, of course, live in the cottage? I know you don't want to close down the business, and if things don't go as you want them to, this way you can return whenever you like. I'll move on and find somewhere else.'

'I couldn't ask you to do that, Jen,' Justin had said, but he had sounded hopeful.

'You didn't. I asked you,' she replied, laughing. 'We'd be doing each other a favour. It would mean I could leave here as soon as I can sort things out and get a flight, and you can go right away, knowing that you don't have to think about closing things down and renting out your cottage or leaving it empty.'

He'd immediately agreed and Jenny had moved back to England, although it had taken a little longer than she'd hoped which meant the bakery, and the cottage, had both stood empty for a few weeks longer than she had planned. It hadn't taken her much time to get things back up and running though and customers soon came flooding back. Now, the queues for Jenny's fare were even longer than they had been for Justin's, or so she had been told by Hettie, and although she'd only lived in the village for less than seven weeks, Jenny was starting to feel that she could be okay here. Not happy, but okay. And that was far better than she thought she'd feel the day she found Silvio in bed with Bianca, the girl who was supposed to have been her best friend.

That was another mistake she wouldn't make again. Believing that someone could be a best friend and be trustworthy, honest, and supportive.

She had believed Bianca had been all of those things … until she found out Bianca had also been sleeping with Silvio.

And Silvio's response when she had eventually plucked up the courage to face him and ask why he was cheating?

'Bella Jenny. I love you both. I love all women. Why can we not all be friends? You, me and Bianca, no?'

'No, Silvio,' Jenny had said.

'I must choose? You ask me to do this?'

'No, Silvio. I'm not asking you to do anything. Other than to go and stick your head in the oven, and to never speak to me again.'

'Mio bambino! Mio bellissimo! Ti amo!'

Jenny sneered at him. 'Don't call me your baby, or beautiful, or say you love me when you've been sleeping with my so-called best friend for the last three months! Yes. Bianca told me. Three months, Silvio. I had no idea. Not a clue. And if I hadn't felt ill and come back to the apartment that day, I wonder how much longer it would've gone on for.'

To which, he'd merely shrugged.

Jenny spotted Mia walking across the green and around the frozen pond, towards the bakery and smiled despite herself and her thoughts. If it hadn't been for Bianca, she could easily have become friends with Mia and Ella. They both seemed lovely and their friendship with one another was clearly deep and genuine. They were true friends to each other. But she couldn't let herself trust anyone again. Not just yet. Not for a long time, possibly. How long did it take to get over being betrayed by both your boyfriend and your best friend? Was there a time period for such things? Or was it, like all other forms of grief, an individual thing? One day you felt as if your life had ended and you remained that way for weeks, or months, or years. Then one day you woke up and things weren't quite so bad. Was that the way it worked? Jenny hoped, in her case, it would be months rather than years. But perhaps you couldn't rush these things. They just happened when they happened. And perhaps, as Hettie Turner had told her shortly after Jenny had arrived, 'It's Fate, deary, and you can't fight your destiny. You're here for a reason. We just don't know what that reason is yet. So why did you leave Florence?'

Jenny smiled again as she remembered that conversation. She hadn't told Hettie, of course, although Hettie hadn't given up trying to find out. And Hettie probably never would, if what other people said about the cheerful, chubby, red-faced woman, were true. Hettie was the village gossip, it seemed. No one managed to keep secrets safe from her. Apart from one woman who had done so. And that was apparently Matilda Ward, Mia's now deceased great-aunt.

Chapter Eight

Jenny walked up the long, snow-covered drive to Little Pond Farm, carrying two large bags containing boxes of cakes and Christmas cookies. She wished she hadn't let Mia talk her into coming tonight. But Mia wouldn't take no for an answer and in the end Jenny had felt it was easier to say yes than continue to try to make excuses. Especially as she had no reason whatsoever not to go to the supper party other than the fact that she didn't want to. She could've simply said that, of course, but even in her head it sounded rude and unfriendly and as miserable as she felt. Jenny didn't want to be either – unless it was absolutely necessary. She'd already turned down Mia's previous invitations to dinner using lame excuses and this time, she hadn't been quick enough to think of one. Hettie Turner popping into the bakery just as Mia was asking hadn't helped matters. Mia on her own was a force to be reckoned with; Mia and Hettie together could've breached the walls of Jericho, no trumpets required.

'It's not so much a supper party,' Mia had said, 'as a thank you meal for anyone coming to help put up decorations at Little Pond Farm. And we need all the help we can get, so you'd really be doing me and Jet a huge favour. Ella and Gill and Mum and Franklin will be there and Hettie and Fred, of course.' She had turned to Hettie who had arrived a second or two before. 'I was going to ask you when you came to clean this morning, Hettie, but as you're here, I'll ask you now.'

'Count us in, deary. I won't be climbing any ladders, but I can decorate a tree and make it a real show stopper. And I'll make some of my cider, shall I?'

'That's exactly what I was going to ask you. And some of those scrumptious mince pies we had yesterday would be fab, if you're feeling up to it.'

'Of course I am, deary. Won't take me long to knock up a batch or two of those.'

'Great. Who else am I asking?' Mia smiled at Jenny. 'Oh yes. Pete, who works at Jet's farm, and Bear, who you may know as Rupert, the vet, will be there.'

'And that man needs cheering up, deary,' Hettie had interjected. 'His girlfriend's just gone to work in China, so they've ended their relationship. Why anyone wants to leave the beautiful English seaside for a smoggy place like that I don't understand, but there it is. Poor dear Rupert doesn't have much luck with the women in his life. Mia dated him, didn't you deary, but she dumped him for Garrick.'

'China has some stunning scenery,' Jenny said, ignoring the gossip she'd already heard. 'I spent six months travelling through parts of Asia before I settled in Florence, and I loved it.'

'Florence is nowhere near Asia, is it deary?' Hettie queried. 'What made you go to Florence? Was it a man? Did you meet some young buck on your travels and follow him to Italy?'

'No,' Jenny said, wishing she hadn't made a comment.

Mia gave both her and Hettie rather odd looks before continuing: 'Anyway. I've asked one or two others. Toby's going to be popping in briefly but he'll have to get back to the pub.'

Hettie tutted. 'Now there's another young man who's not so lucky in love, my dears. His girlfriend's just dumped him because of all that nasty business with his sister. Doesn't want to be dating a relative of a convicted criminal, apparently.'

'I didn't know that,' Mia said. 'That he'd been dumped, I mean. I just saw him in the lane and he didn't mention it.'

'I don't think he's told anyone yet, deary. Freda heard them having a bit of a barney over the phone last night. The girlfriend called him on the pub landline and said her parents weren't happy about her relationship with him.' Hettie rolled her eyes. 'She's in her thirties, deary. Surely she can make her own decisions? But who needs someone like that in their life, my dears? He's better off without her, as I'm sure he'll come to see in time. These things happen for a reason, dears. Poor dear Toby. He's such a sweet young man. Nothing like that dreadful sister of his. Why do people think they can lump everyone together and tar them with the same brush? Just because one person acts in a particular way, it doesn't mean everyone else will, does it dears? I judge each person on their own merits, or lack of them. And Prince Gustav's a good judge of character, you know. If he likes you, it's as certain as nine pence that I'll like you too. Although I try to see good in everyone. Never took to the last vicar though. Actually bit him.'

'You bit the vicar?' Jenny was astonished. She knew Hettie was a bit 'out there' but biting a vicar was a step too far.

Mia sniggered but Hettie looked at Jenny as if she had a screw loose.

'Not me, deary. Prince Gustav. Although I was very tempted to give the so and so a good clip around the ear once or twice. The vicar, not my darling Prince Gustav.'

'I see,' Jenny said. 'Um. I must get on. I know it doesn't look busy in here this morning, and a lot of people are staying home, due to the snow I expect, but I do have things to do. Sorry. Lovely chatting with you both though. May I tempt you with anything before you go?'

'Oh. Well. Just a loaf of your wonderful soda bread for me, deary,' Hettie said, frowning slightly.

'And I'll have three of your iced cinnamon swirls,' Mia said, cheerfully. 'Plus your promise that you'll come tonight and bring a selection of your delicious cakes. For which I'll pay, of course. I won't take no for an answer, so please say you'll come. We're beginning to think you don't like us, or that we've done something wrong. Let us show you we're just a friendly bunch of people who want to enjoy the festive season.'

'Your dear cousin Justin joined in with everything,' Hettie said, scowling a little at Jenny. 'He was a real part of this village. We all hoped you'd be the same, deary, but if we're not good enough for you, well, that's that.' Hettie pursed her lips and clasped her hands beneath her ample bosom, the loaf of soda bread, now squashed against her chest.

Jenny had been talked into a corner. 'Of course you're good enough and it's not that I don't like you, or that anyone has done anything wrong. It's simply that I'm rather shy, and besides, I don't like Christmas. I never have.'

'Shy? Someone who's travelled around Asia and lived and worked in Florence can't be that shy,' Mia had said, with a friendly smile. 'And not liking Christmas is even more reason you should come. Ella and I love Christmas and before tonight is over, I can promise you, you won't dislike it nearly as much. We'll see you at six-thirty. Bye.'

Jenny hadn't been able to think of a retort by the time Mia had bustled Hettie out of the door, so here she was, walking towards Jet's farmhouse, in the freezing cold.

The ground still had a blanket of snow from last night, parts of which had turned to ice, and as it was virtually pitch black save for a shaft of pale moonlight, she had to watch where she was walking. She'd foolishly forgotten to charge her phone, so she couldn't even use the torch beam on that. As mobile phone reception was non-existent in the village, she often forgot to charge the thing these days.

She was definitely feeling grumpy. It had been only slightly above freezing all day, and every time the door of the bakery had opened and closed, a gust of bitterly cold air had slapped her in the face, no matter where she had stood to try to avoid it. It was as if even the wind was taunting her and now, with every step she took she came closer to what she was sure would be an evening of pure hell.

In the silence of the evening, she heard the ice crunch behind her. Someone – or something – was hurrying towards her. She spun round to see a tall, broad figure gaining ground, but in the darkness, she couldn't make out his face and the beam of his torch was almost blinding her.

'Jenny?' the man said, just as she had decided that it must be a guest for the supper party and not, as she had first imagined, a serial killer stalking her, but she didn't recognise the voice.

'Yes,' she tentatively replied, shielding her eyes from the light. 'Who is it?'

He came closer as he spoke and lowered the torch. 'It's Bear. I mean, it's Rupert. Rupert Day. The village vet.'

She breathed a sigh of relief and took a step forward but as she did so, her boot heel caught on a piece of ice and she slipped. She would have fallen had it not been for his quick reactions. She suddenly found herself enveloped in a pair of strong arms, and felt warm breath on her cheek. A whiff of sandalwood aftershave and a very sexy smile made her sigh unexpectedly. What on earth was wrong with her?

'Are you okay?' His voice held concern but also a hint of laughter.

She found her footing and straightened up, easing herself away from him and out of his arms.

'I'm fine, thank you. Thanks for saving me from falling.'

'Anytime,' he said, smiling rather sexily as his torch scanned her from head to toe and back again. 'You look lovely tonight. I think I've only seen you once or twice since you moved here, and you've always been half-hidden behind your counter.'

'Thank you.' She tugged the belt of her bottle-green winter coat more tightly about her waist. 'I'm not one for socialising, so I haven't been to the pub. I prefer bed and a good book.'

He grinned. 'I'm with you on the bed front. The book, not so much.'

'Oh. Why are you called Bear?' she asked, quickly changing the subject.

'Everyone asks me that, but it's not for the reason most people think. Mum and Dad met on a bear watching trip in Canada, where they did more than watch bears because I was born nine months later, by which time they had at least had the decency to get married. To mark the occasion, they gave me Bear as a middle name. Rupert was my grandfather so my name is Rupert Bear Day. I got plenty of stick at school for that, I can tell you. Parents don't realise the damage they do to their kids by giving them odd names.' He gave a burst of laughter. 'But I am nice to cuddle up to on a cold night such as this one.'

He was also one of the biggest flirts she had ever met and she made a mental note to avoid him at all costs for the rest of the evening. But for now, she could benefit from his torch.

'I've never been to Canada,' she said. 'But I have seen Pandas in China. They're well worth watching. Shall we continue to the house together?'

He grinned. 'It would seem silly not to. China, eh? I'm impressed.' He held out his arm for her.

'My girlfriend, or I should say, ex-girlfriend's just gone there.'

'Yes. So I heard. I'm fine thanks,' she said, ignoring his arm and leaving a gap between them as they moved forward.

'I can see that. But it's very icy here and you've already slipped once. I promise I'll be a perfect gentleman. Let me carry your bags.'

She hesitated but with her next step, she felt her foot slide again and quickly handed him one of her bags, linking her arm through his. 'Thank you.'

'There,' he said, and she knew he was grinning broadly even though she didn't look at his face. 'This isn't so bad, is it?'

Chapter Nine

Glen was coming back out of the farmhouse with four more boxes of lights that Mia had given him when he saw Jenny arrive, arm in arm with Rupert. Jet, who was standing a few feet away from Glen, called out to his friend.

'Hi Bear. Oh. Hi Jenny. Glad you could make it. Mia's inside. May I grab Bear from you? We could use an extra pair of hands.'

'We're not together,' Jenny said, looking both surprised and embarrassed, Glen noticed. And he recognised the feeling of relief that swept over him. For one awful moment there, he had thought Jenny might be dating Bear.

Bear didn't seem bothered. He handed Jenny back her bag, winked at her and headed towards Jet.

'Hi Jenny.' Glen smiled at her and was pleased that she returned it.

'Hello. Gosh, It's so cold tonight. Rather you than me.' She nodded her head towards the boxes in his arms and the tumble of lights already draped across an ornate bench beside the portico. A pile of light-up candy canes lay on the floor and two large Norway Spruce leant against the aged sandstone façade of the Georgian farmhouse.

'We've got our work cut out.' He grinned and put the boxes of lights on the bench. 'Mia wants lights around these stone pillars and I must admit, as much as I'm not really into Christmas decorations, they will add a touch of welcome to this portico.'

'And the candy canes?' Jenny raised her brows, amusement flickering in her hazel eyes.

'Ah yes. The candy canes. I believe they're going to line part of the driveway. Although I think Jet said he could think of somewhere else he'd like to stick them.' He laughed and she laughed with him.

Still smiling, Jenny moved forward. 'I'd better let you get on or you'll be here all night. Mia's inside, I believe Jet said?'

He stepped aside to let her pass, breathing in her scent of winter spices. Or perhaps that was from the boxes of cakes she clearly had in her bags.

'Yes. She's in the kitchen with Ella, Gill, Lori and Hettie. It's the second door on your right, but you'll hear the laughter long before you find the door.'

He almost hadn't come tonight but now he was very glad he had. When Mia had called at his cottage this morning and said they were having a Christmas decorating supper party, he knew it meant the entire evening would be gone. He had so much to do, what with re-instating the choir, organising the charity carol evening, preparing sermons and the services for Christmas aside from a whole list of other things requiring his attention. But Mia, Jet and their friends were some of the few people in the village around his age and he had rather enjoyed helping decorate Hettie and Fred's cottage yesterday. One evening wouldn't hurt. And when Mia mentioned that Jenny would be bringing cakes, his mind was made up. Not that it was really Jenny's cakes that interested him.

'She's prettier than I thought, close up,' Bear was telling Jet, Franklin and Pete as Glen went to join them. 'And that hair of hers. I wouldn't mind getting my hands tangled in that.'

Glen stiffened. He liked discussing women as much as any of them but he didn't like the way Bear was talking about Jenny.

'Shall I start on the portico lights?' he asked.

Jet, who along with the others was filling one of two massive lead-like, square planters with soil, nodded. 'If you're okay with that, yes please. There's a stepladder in the back of that Land Rover.' He tipped his head in the direction of the battered-looking vehicle. 'And there're some of those weatherproof stick-on hooks on the bench, or maybe the windowsill. Mia says they'll last in most conditions but I don't see how. Unless they stick so firmly that half the plaster comes off the wall when you remove them. I can see I'll probably have to have the place repainted, inside and out when these decorations come down.'

Bear frowned. 'Why put them up if you don't want them?'

Jet shook his head and grinned. 'Mia wants them.'

'So what?' Bear said. 'It's your house.'

'Mia's probably going to be staying here for a couple of weeks. I want her to feel at home, and if decorations make her happy, that's a small price to pay.'

Bear smirked. 'You've really gone soft since you've been seeing her.'

Jet stopped shovelling soil and looked Bear in the eye. 'It's called Love, Bear, and to be completely honest with you, I've never been happier in my life. You should try it. I can thoroughly recommend it. And believe me, I never thought those words would ever come out of my mouth.'

'I'll second that,' Franklin said, grinning. 'I'm a changed man since I met Lori.'

'Yeah,' Bear said. 'You're even losing that Texan drawl you had. I'm not sure I want some woman changing my life or my behaviour. What about you, Glen? Would you change your ways for a woman?'

'For the right woman, yes. But it's not necessarily about changing, is it? It's about another person bringing out the best in you, and hopefully, you bringing out the best in them.'

'That's it exactly,' Jet said, smiling at him. 'Although I have changed, I think. I was so angry about my dad before I met Mia, and I'd got stuck in a way of life that wasn't good for me. Mia helped me see that. Or falling in love with her did. I realised I wanted a relationship with her. A serious relationship and that meant I had to change the way I thought about certain things. But Mia didn't change me. I changed myself. And it was because I wanted to. When you meet the right woman, Bear, you'll want to do the same, I suspect.'

Pete nodded. 'I'd go along with that. But it has to be the right one. You think you're immune and then, wham! Love smashes you in the face and you're a gonna.'

'How romantic!' It was Ella's voice and Glen and the others all turned around as she carried a tray of mugs out of the house; steam rising from each one.

Glen smiled. 'Hettie's hot, spiced cider punch?'

Ella nodded. 'We thought you men might need warming up, and possibly a break from all the hard work, but there doesn't seem to be much work going on.' She grinned and handed the tray to Glen. 'I would stay and supervise but it's freezing out here.'

'You're right about that,' Bear said. 'It is freezing.'

'Then stop gossiping and get on with it. Supper will be ready in an hour and you haven't even got one set of lights up yet. When Gill's finished in the kitchen, I'll send him out to help.' She hurried back inside, closing the front door behind her.

'I see what you mean,' Bear said, sarcasm written all over his face as well as in his tone. 'I've clearly never been in love. I can't wait to find 'The One' and be ordered around by her. Gill's a very lucky man. You all are. Oh. Apart from you, Glen. You obviously need to fall madly in love too.'

After seeing Jenny again tonight, Glen was certain he was already halfway there.

Chapter Ten

Mia was very pleased with how the evening was going apart from the fact that Little M had got herself entangled in a string of fairy lights, tried to eat a robin ornament and almost got hold of the plate of turkey Gill had prepared to go in the curry. It had also taken Jet and the other men a little longer to complete the outdoor decorations than Mia had expected, especially after Little M was banished outside with them. But together with the rest of the girls – and she included Hettie and Fred amongst the girls on this occasion – the indoor decorations were finished with time to spare before the turkey Thai curry was due to be ready.

There would be thirteen people seated around the table, where Mia had carefully placed name cards to ensure that everyone sat exactly where she wanted them to. She had put Jet at the head of the table, naturally, and she would be sitting to his right. Jenny would be to his left and Glen beside

Jenny, with Ella next to Glen. Then Gill, and beside him, Hettie, who would be next to Fred. Lori and Franklin were to sit beside Mia; Bear beside Pete, whose wife was a nurse and couldn't make this evening due to being on shift, then Toby, who arrived just in time to help put the finishing touches to the outdoor decorations.

'Now that Bear and Toby are single again,' Mia said, as Ella placed the last of the wine glasses, Christmas crackers and intricately folded napkins on the table, 'we really need to find more single women. It's a pity Anna's gone to Tenerife for Christmas, or I would've invited her.'

Ella grinned. 'Has she forgiven you for Jet? She seemed pretty upset when we all went out for drinks the day you told her.'

'I think so. Although I haven't seen her or any of the girls I met on the beach, for weeks. But the rest of them have kids and I know they're rushed off their feet at the moment.'

'Do we know any other single women?' Ella scattered a mixture of tiny red and silver glittery stars along the entire length of the extended, antique mahogany table.

'No. And that's the problem. I was hoping to get Jenny and Glen together in time for Christmas, but now that Bear and Toby are available again she may prefer one of them.'

'Bear's lovely to look at, with his black hair and rugby-fit body, but we both know he's a flirt, and sex-mad. Not that that's a problem, but he isn't terribly romantic either, is he? I get the feeling Jenny could do with a bit of romance.'

'I thought that too. Toby's more romantic.'

'True. But he's also got red hair. Not as red as Jenny's but even so. Could you imagine their kids?' Ella pulled a face.

'Don't be mean. There's nothing wrong with redheads.'

'Except they get called all sorts of names at school, like gingernut, for example. Kids can be cruel.'

'Gingernut isn't that bad. I love gingernut biscuits. But Jenny's hair is so dark, it's more burnt copper than ginger.'

'Then they'll be called conkerhead or something. Why Jenny and Glen? Just because you thought they were the only singletons in the village at the time?'

Mia shook her head and met Ella's eyes. 'Not just because of that. Hettie thinks Glen's keen on Jenny, and so do I.'

'Really? What makes you think that? The poor guy's only been here two weeks and Hettie's started gossiping about him already.' Ella shook her head but she was grinning. 'But his post here's only temporary. He may be gone before the end of January. Is it wise to throw two people together if we already know one of them won't be staying?'

Mia stood back and admired the table, grinning at Ella when she was satisfied it looked precisely as she'd hoped. 'He might change his mind and stay. If he had someone to stay for.'

Ella laughed. 'He told us yesterday, after a few glasses of Hettie's cider, that he was only here as a favour to his uncle, the Bishop, and that this was his first posting to a village. He didn't look thrilled. And Gill told me they were talking about London when they were on the roof because Gill mentioned he was taking us to the ballet in the New Year. Glen apparently said he loved London and was hoping his next position would be there, or some other large city. I can't see him staying.'

Mia spotted a spoon a fraction out of place and quickly realigned it. 'Remember how we felt when we came here. We were dreading it, but look at us now. Would either of us leave unless we had to? I know I wouldn't.'

Ella shrugged. 'That's true. Look. Here come the others.'

Everyone piled into the dining room, the men from outside, the others from either the direction of the kitchen, or the sitting room, where more decorations had been put up. After taking a quick look around the room, Jet went straight to Mia, pulled her into his arms and kissed her.

'I was wrong,' he said, when he released her. 'I wasn't keen on having decorations inside and out. At least, nowhere near so many. But the whole place looks beautiful. Thank you.' He looked around the room and smiled. 'And thank you all for helping.'

'I'm only here for the curry,' Toby said. 'But Jet's right, Mia. I've never seen this place look so festive, even when Mrs Cross was alive. Your mum loved Christmas, didn't she, Jet?'

Jet nodded and kept his arm around Mia, squeezing her to him. 'She did. And she would've loved this. All of it.'

'Even the light-up candy canes?' Ella asked, both her grin and her voice dripping with sarcasm.

Jet grinned at her. 'Even those. Are we going to have a big switch on of all the lights before we eat?'

'I want to see what you've done outside,' Mia said. 'Especially the trees. Gill? Do we have time to go and see the lights and have a glass of champagne?'

Gill nodded. 'I can leave supper to simmer and keep the rice warm in the steamer for another five or ten minutes.'

'Great,' Jet said. 'Come on everyone. I'll get the champagne from the fridge.'

'Ella's put a tray of glasses in the hall,' Mia said. 'Let's go and grab our coats, go outside, and officially turn on the lights.'

Less than three minutes later, everyone stood on the drive of Little Pond Farm facing the aged sandstone façade of the Georgian farmhouse. A glass of champagne in their hands, they were all wrapped warmly in their coats, gloves and scarves, and all wearing Santa hats which Ella had handed out to everyone. Even Little M had a hat perched jauntily on her head. She seemed very keen on catching the white bobble at the tip of it, in her mouth.

They counted down from ten, and Jet flicked the outside switch the second they said, 'One.' Mia felt tears well up in her eyes and when she glanced at Ella, Ella had them too.

'It's like a winter wonderland, deary,' Hettie said. 'I'm getting all emotional.'

'Me too,' Mia said, stretching up to kiss Jet on the lips when he came back and stood beside her, while everyone else 'ooh-ed' and 'ahh-ed' at the gorgeous display.

The Norway Spruce now stood either side of the white portico in the lead effect square planters which Mia had specifically bought for them that day; strings of delicate white lights were draped around the trees and twinkling brightly. Identical lights were wrapped around the columns of the portico and across the arch between. On the black front door, hung a wreath of holly, evergreen, poinsettia, shiny red baubles and sparkly frosted white ones, all interlaced with a wide, red ribbon tied in a large bow at the top. The antique lamp hanging from its hook in the centre of the portico ceiling held a realistic but battery-lit large candle, glowing warm white in the shadows. More white lights were strung along the fences either side of the house, and the light-up candy canes began at the top of the drive and ended halfway down just before the wooden gate, which was also strung with lights.

'No snowmen?' Ella queried, grinning at Jet.

'They melted,' he replied, with a wink. 'But we have put some of those twig reindeer beside the path leading to the barns.' He pointed to the right.

Mia and Ella both rushed to look, and there they were; four reindeer, just like the ones on the roof of Sunbeam Cottage, covered in white lights, with bunches of holly around their necks stood on the snow-covered grass beside the path leading from the drive to the barns and the farmyard.

'They look so cute,' Ella said, smiling gleefully.

'It's a pity they're not real,' Mia replied.

Ella glanced at her, an excited look on her face. 'They could be. You're rich. You could hire real reindeer for Christmas. Think how great that would be.'

'Er. Excuse me,' Jet said, coming to stand beside Mia. 'Real reindeer? I thought you didn't like farm animals.'

'Reindeer aren't farm animals.' Mia linked her arm through his. 'They're Christmas animals.'

'The Sámi may disagree with you about that.' He smiled down at her. 'Oh God. I'm going to be having reindeer, aren't I?'

'Would you mind?'

He sighed and shook his head. 'I suppose not. But only if you agree to help look after them. And

I have no idea where one goes to shop for reindeer. And don't say the North Pole, Ella.'

Ella laughed. 'Google will know.'

Mia flung her arms around Jet's neck and planted kisses all over his face. 'You're the best boyfriend any girl could wish for. I love you, Jet Cross. Come on. Let's tell everyone we're getting reindeer.'

Oddly enough, no one seemed particularly surprised, other than Jenny and Glen.

'Reindeer?' Glen said. 'Real, living, breathing reindeer?'

'Do you need a permit for those?' Jenny asked.

Mia stood beaming at them. 'I've no idea if you need a permit. But I know there are reindeer farms in England, and I'm sure there's one in Kent or Sussex, so we'll soon find out. Ooh. Perhaps we can hire someone with specialist knowledge to come and look after them. Gosh. It really is wonderful being rich.'

'And if we get the really heavy snow they forecast,' Ella said, 'we could hire a sleigh and drive around the village in it. This is going to be a fabulous Christmas. But it's freezing out here. Let's turn on the indoor lights and then eat. I'm starving.'

'Excellent plan,' Gill said, and Mia and Jet followed their guests inside.

'Reindeer,' Jet said, shaking his head and chuckling. 'I'm going to have to clear out one of the storage barns to make room for them. And find out what reindeer eat. And God knows where we'll find a place for a sleigh. If anyone had told me this time last year that I'd be talking about such things, I'd have laughed in their face and told them they were mad.'

'We don't have to do it,' Mia said, smiling at him as they walked into the hall. 'It's a nice idea but it'll probably be a lot of work, and I honestly don't mind if you'd rather not have more animals running around.'

'Nope.' He grinned at her. 'I quite like the idea of having reindeer. Now, let's see what you girls have done in here.'

Everyone had already seen the tree in the hall, festooned with red gossamer ribbons and sparkling red baubles, gold poinsettia leaves, heavenly scented bunches of cinnamon sticks tied with red ribbon and myriad twinkling white lights. The decorations of evergreen intertwined with more white lights and red ribbon trailed up the banisters, but when Jet walked into the sitting room, Mia heard his sharp intake of breath.

'Do you like it?' She looked into his eyes, a little nervously.

'I love it.' His voice cracked with emotion and she could see from the expression on his face that he was genuinely happy.

She entwined her fingers with his. 'I remembered seeing a photo of this very room at Christmas, which Mattie must have taken when your mum was still alive. I used all the decorations in the box you gave me from the attic, but Ella and I bought some today in town that we couldn't find in the box. I wanted it to be as close as possible to the photo.' She picked up the photo from a side table and handed it to him. She had printed it out that morning and taken it with her to the shops. 'I thought it might make us feel as if your mum was sharing Christmas with us.'

The log fire crackled in the huge hearth while Jet scanned the room and Mia watched him as if only they were here and none of the guests.

'I remember this so well,' he said, looking and sounding very emotional, but in a good way. 'It was the year Mattie lent me the money to buy this place. Our first Christmas in this farmhouse. Mattie bought the tree, and she took Mum into town to buy more decorations without telling me. They spent the rest of the day baking mince pies and shortbread, sausage rolls, cheese straws and cinnamon biscuits with red and green sprinkles.' He laughed cheerily. 'I came in from a long day in the fields to a roaring fire, just like this. The tree, with pine cones, dried orange and lemon slices pinned with cloves, those cinnamon sticks, the multi-coloured lights and those red, white and silver ribbons, bells and bows. This is it exactly. Even the evergreen on the mantle and the candles – although ours were real. I take it these ones are battery operated.'

Mia nodded and smiled. 'Safety first. The only things I couldn't find were the Christmas stockings. But I did find the hooks. So if it's okay with you, we'll buy new stockings tomorrow. Unless you know where they are.'

'I think I do.' He turned to face her, his eyes full of love and his smile overflowing with warmth and thanks. 'But let's buy new ones for us. Mum would like that.'

'Oh God,' Ella said, wiping her eyes. 'This is so emotional.'

'Imagine how I feel,' Jet said, not taking his eyes from Mia's face for a second. 'I love you, Mia Ward. And I'm so glad Mattie wanted us to be together. I owe your great-aunt more than I can ever say.'

'You and me both,' Mia said, as Jet bent his head to kiss her.

Chapter Eleven

Jenny was feeling happier than she had for a long time. The supper party last night was far better than she expected and she actually enjoyed herself. What's more, Mia had insisted on paying for the cakes Jenny took with her, which meant Jenny had not only had an evening of fun, laughter, delicious food and copious amounts of wine, all in good company, but she had also made money. Who wouldn't be happy about that?

Even when it had started snowing again as she and the others had walked home, it didn't sour her mood. Mia had stayed at Jet's, of course, and Lori and Franklin had returned to their farm cottage, and Pete to his, but everyone else had walked back through the village saying good night along the way as each reached their doors. Only she, Glen, Toby and Bear, continued farther on, but as Toby and Bear were in deep conversation regarding Toby's sister, Jenny and Glen had time to talk.

'Tonight was fun,' Glen said, his hands stuffed into his coat pockets, the Santa hat still sitting skewed on his thick, blond hair, and his cheeks almost as red as the hat. 'But it's so cold. Be careful where you're walking. There are several icy patches on this part of the lane.'

Jenny smiled at him, thankful that such a tiny village as this not only had streetlights, but also multi-coloured Christmas lights strung between each lamppost, making it much easier to see where she was walking. She had almost slipped again, coming down Jet's drive, but Gill had offered his free arm, Ella already clasping the other. When they reached Sunbeam Cottage and said good night to Ella and Gill, Bear had once more offered his, as had Glen, but Jenny had said she would be fine, now that she could see the path before her.

'Thanks.' She avoided a treacherous looking spot and smiled again at Glen. 'You're right. Tonight was fun. To be honest, I wasn't looking forward to it, but I'm very glad I went. Mia and Jet are so in love, aren't they? It almost restores my faith in romance.'

'Oh?' He raised a brow. 'Does your faith need restoring? On the romance front?'

She gave a little cough, threw him a brief glance from under her lashes, and sighed. 'I don't think that's possible, unfortunately.'

'I remember you saying that your boyfriend in Florence broke your heart. I thought it was a figure of speech. Was it more serious than that? Would you like to talk about it? I'm a good listener.'

She let out a little peal of laughter, but it didn't sound jolly even to her ears. 'Thanks. But no thanks. The less said about it, the better, as far as I'm concerned. I just want to put the whole thing behind me, forget it, and get on with my life.'

'And are you? Getting on with your life?'

She felt, rather than saw, his gaze on her, and she shrugged. 'I'm trying. I couldn't believe my luck when Justin told me he was moving away. I immediately asked if I could come and take over the bakery, and when he said yes, and that I could even change the name, I thought it would be a whole new start for me. And it has been. But I've never lived in a village before and … well, let's just say living in a fishbowl would probably be less public.'

Glen laughed, and it was the kind of laugh that brought a smile to your face whether you wanted it to or not. A warm, friendly sound, full of hope and promise.

'I know exactly how you feel. I was born in a village, not a million miles away from here in fact, and no matter what I did, it seemed that someone had seen me do it, and was eager to tell my dad. He was a vicar too. Still is. But he and Mum are living in China now.'

'China? I backpacked through parts of China. It's a beautiful place, and I was only talking to Mia and Hettie about it this morning because Bear's girlfriend has just moved there.'

'What a small world!'

'Did someone say my name?' Bear asked, glancing over his shoulder and grinning.

'We were talking about China,' Jenny replied.

'Oh.' Bear frowned and shook his head. 'Everyone seems to be talking about China recently. I told you about my girlfriend, didn't I, Glen? And if I didn't, I know Hettie would've done. Or I should say, ex-girlfriend. It's probably just as well she's gone. Things weren't working out. And now I'm young, free and single again.' He winked at Jenny, and gave her a devilish grin, which she ignored. 'I'm going to the pub with Toby. You two fancy joining us?'

'No thanks,' Jenny replied, perhaps rather too quickly. 'It's been a long day, and I've got an early start again tomorrow. I'll say good night now because I'm heading across the green.'

'I'll walk you to your door,' Glen immediately said, before replying to Bear's invitation. 'I think I've had enough to drink tonight, thanks all the same.'

'Thank you.' Jenny meant to add that it really wasn't necessary for him to walk her home as it was only a matter of yards, but somehow the rest of the sentence didn't reach her lips, and instead, she merely smiled.

'See you around then,' Bear said, giving a half-hearted wave.

'Good night,' said Toby, smiling warmly. 'See you tomorrow, Glen.'

'Good night,' Glen replied with a friendly wave before turning his attention to Jenny and once again offering his arm. 'It's harder to see the ice on the grass. I'd hate you to fall over this close to home.'

She nodded and linked her arm through his. 'What's happening tomorrow?' She hadn't meant to ask that, and had no idea why she had. 'Not that it's any of my business. Sorry.'

'No need to be sorry. It's choir practice. I've reinstated the choir. I mentioned it yesterday.'

'Did you? Gosh. I don't remember. I do remember you mentioning the charity carol singing on Saturday, though.'

He grinned. 'I believe you said you make a dog sound like a prima donna.'

She laughed. 'I did, and I do. Believe me.'

'So just come along and mime. You said you didn't want to go tonight, but you had fun. Come on Saturday evening. You might enjoy yourself more than you think.'

They had reached her door and she stopped and turned to face him. 'I might. That's possible. May I think about it and let you know?'

'Of course. And I'll see you tomorrow, if there's anything you want to ask.'

'Tomorrow? I'm not coming to choir practice, Glen.'

'I know. But I'll be coming here tomorrow. It seems I've got a bit of an addiction to the things you bake.'

'Oh. Well, I'll look forward to it.'

For a brief moment, they stared into each other's eyes, while soft, white flakes of snow fell silently around them. Somewhere in the distance an owl hooted and a vixen screamed to her mate, but all Jenny could think about was how blue Glen's eyes were, and how eminently kissable his mouth looked right now.

'Good night, Jenny. God bless.'

'Good night, Glen. Pleasant dreams.'

'I'll see you tomorrow then?'

'Yes, Glen. Until tomorrow.'

She quickly turned away, unlocked the door and closed it behind her before she did something she might live to regret.

Chapter Twelve

Nothing could ruin Glen's mood today. Not even Hettie Turner. Last night he was sure he had seen something in Jenny's eyes that gave him hope, and when he had gone to bed he had dreamt the most wonderful dream. He was living in a vicarage, covered with wisteria, while a large flock of chickens and an equally large brood of children ran freely and gleefully around a flower-filled garden. Jenny sat beside him on a wicker loom chair, pouring tea from a porcelain teapot into matching porcelain cups, and plates on the wicker table overflowed with a selection of Jenny's delicious cakes.

When he first woke up, he wasn't sure what had surprised him the most about the dream. That the vicarage seemed to be in the middle of nowhere; certainly not a town, and definitely not a city, and, aside from the wisteria, had looked a lot like the cottage he lived in now. That he and Jenny appeared to be the parents of a great number of children. Or that they kept chickens. He was still thinking about it as Hettie was rebuking him.

'There's not much point in holding choir practice, vicar,' Hettie said. 'If you've forgotten to ask the organist to come. It's been several weeks since the last one and no one will remember the tunes.'

'I'm sure we'll be able to make do,' Glen said, with a friendly smile.

'Make do? I would've thought you'd want to make a good impression for the Bishop. I've heard rumours, you know. If this place doesn't get back on its feet, this parish may be merged with one of the other villages. We can't have that, vicar. This church has been here since September 29th 1018. It says so on the foundation stone. Although the village has been here much longer than that. Alfred the Great stayed here, you know. But Little Pondale without St Michael and All Angels is unthinkable, vicar. The diocese won't leave it empty, will they? They'll probably try to sell the place off to recoup some of the money the last vicar embezzled. Some obnoxious property dealer will turn the place into luxury flats and charge a fortune for them. There'll be fast cars, and even faster women tearing about the place. And what about the Angel Bell? Been here for centuries that has. Dear Matilda paid to have the belfry restored to make sure it was here for generations to come. What will happen to that? Sold off and melted down? And all because you forgot to send an email to the organist.'

'I take your point, Hettie,' Glen said, trying desperately hard not to laugh. 'I'll call the organist right now. And then I must go and get some cakes for this evening. I thought it would be a nice touch.'

Hettie linked her hands beneath her bosom and beamed at him. 'Nice touch indeed. I wasn't born yesterday. You can tell me, vicar. You've got a glint in your eye for our young Jenny, haven't you? I saw the two of you last night. If you'd like me to put in a good word, I'm happy to do that. But only if you plan to stay. Can't have you breaking the poor girl's heart. I'm pretty sure that's what happened to her in Florence. That's why she's here, you know. To get over a disappointment in love. Do you plan to stay, vicar?'

'I don't know,' he said, after thinking about it for a moment. 'I honestly don't know.'

'Well then, we'll just have to see how things go, won't we? I believe in destiny, you know. I mean, look at me and Fred. If dear Matilda hadn't put that clause in her will, meaning Mia had to come here to live, Lori wouldn't have come to stay and started the book club, and I wouldn't have met Fred. Destiny, you see.'

'Or God's plan, perhaps, don't you think?'

She pursed her lips. 'Well, I don't know about God's plan, but I do know about the Wishing Tree, if you want to give destiny a bit of a helping hand.'

'Excuse me? The Wishing Tree?'

Hettie nodded. 'Yes. The Wishing Tree. It's halfway up Frog Hill, fairly close to Frog's Hollow. That's the pond where everyone goes skinny-dipping on Midsummer's Night. But don't go there on a Monday.'

Glen shook his head. This was getting confusing. 'I'm sorry? Why shouldn't I go there on a Monday?'

'Why, because of the curse, of course. The curse of Frog's Hollow. Has no one mentioned it?'

'No. And there's no need, Hettie because I don't believe in curses.'

'Neither did my Hector. But a car hit him, tossed him in the air, and he landed on his head. Dead as a dodo. And all because he went to Frog's Hollow on a Monday.'

'Hector was your first husband, is that right? I'm sorry for your loss.'

'Oh don't be, vicar. Hector stayed with me for years after. Until I married Fred, in fact. Hector gave me away on my wedding day. Moved on to his next life, now he has. I miss him. But he couldn't hang around forever, could he, vicar? But I was telling you about the Wishing Tree.'

Glen blinked several times. What was Hettie going on about?

'Ah yes. The Wishing Tree.'

'Now it only works in December, so you haven't got that long. And if it's love you're looking for, with a particular person, you need to write their name on something and tie it to the tree or place it at its base. No pins, mind. You mustn't go sticking things in the Wishing Tree. How would you like it if someone came and stuck a pin in you, vicar? So you leave it at the tree, or tie it to a branch and then you make a wish.'

She beamed at him, and he waited for her to continue, but she didn't.

'That's it?'

She nodded. 'That's it.'

'So a person could be waiting around forever for their wish to come true.' He couldn't help grinning now.

'Oh, good heavens no, vicar. The wish will come true in seven days, if the tree decides you're worthy.'

He raised his brows. 'If the *tree* decides?'

'Of course, vicar. Trees are living too, you know. And most of them have been around for a lot longer than us. Trees are wise. The Wishing Tree, more wise than most.'

'Thank you, Hettie. I'll bear that in mind. Now if you'll excuse me, I've got an organist to call, and some cakes to buy.'

'And I must go and give Prince Gustav and Fred their lunch. Remember, vicar, the tree only works in December.'

'I don't think I'll forget, Hettie. I'm sure I'll be thinking about this conversation for days to come.'

He walked towards the church door, shaking his head as he did so. One thing he could safely say about Little Pondale was that it certainly had some characters.

And it also had the most beautiful woman he was sure he had ever seen.

London might have people as odd as Hettie, but it didn't have Jenny Lake, and as ridiculous as it was, it seemed that Jenny was racing up his list of requirements for a possible, future posting.

Chapter Thirteen

Cathy Cole pulled up outside Corner Cottage and yanked on her handbrake.

'Are we there yet?' her six-year-old daughter, Daisy asked, raising her head to peer out the window, but keeping her earbuds firmly in place.

'Yes, honey,' Cathy's best friend, Christy replied, nodding her head. 'Is Dylan awake?'

'What?' Daisy asked, still not removing her earbuds.

Christy pointed at the little girl slumped beside Daisy and mouthed the words with emphasis as well as saying them. 'I think you mean, pardon. And I asked if Dylan is awake?'

Daisy merely shrugged and Cathy sighed, smiling at Christy. 'Sometimes you can get more sense out of a turnip than you can from my child.' She glanced out the window at the snow-covered cottage, one of a row of several along the length of a narrow but quaint little lane. 'This place looks just as it did in the photos on the website, doesn't it? Only it wasn't covered in snow. I'm so excited about this, Christy. I know we've all been through some rough times lately, but this Christmas is going to be great. I'm sure of it.'

'I'm not sure I like the owner's taste in Christmas decorations,' Christy said, leaning across Cathy to look out at the cottage. 'Are those light-up candy canes? And is that really a plastic snowman on the lawn?'

Cathy grinned. 'There's one on the roof too.'

'Dear God.' Christy collapsed back in her seat. 'Kill me now.'

Cathy nudged her arm. 'The inside looked a bit old-fashioned but rather twee from the photos. Perhaps the owner thought we'd like these decorations because we've got young kids.'

'Hmm. So where do we have to go to get the key?'

'To Sunbeam Cottage.' Cathy grabbed her phone from the built-in charger plate and looked at the screen. 'The woman was right about phone reception, look. Absolutely zilch.'

'At least that means we'll get some peace and quiet. If he can't get through on the mobile, and you didn't tell him where we were going, he can't keep pestering you. I suppose coming to the back of beyond has an upside.'

'Shush!' Cathy put her finger to her lips. 'Not in front of Daisy.'

'Daisy can't hear a word. But sorry, I forgot. So where's this cottage then?'

'A few doors up, I think the woman said. I'll drive slowly and you keep an eye out for the name. She did say it was a big yellow cottage about halfway up Lily Pond Lane.'

'Well, this is Lily Pond Lane and I can see the pond. Oh. I can also see a yellow cottage from here. And oh dear God. It's got the same snowman on the roof. And … reindeer. Four, twig-looking reindeer. I simply can't wait to meet this woman. I can almost picture her now.'

'Perhaps she's got kids too.' Cathy released the handbrake and drove towards Sunbeam Cottage, narrowly avoiding a chubby, red-faced woman who appeared from nowhere, two cottages down. 'Sorry,' she shouted, raising her hand in a gesture of apology, but the woman merely glared at her and hurried across the lane and over the snow-blanketed, village green.

'Don't kill one of the locals the minute we arrive,' Christy said, a huge grin spreading across her lips.

Cathy stopped outside the cottage. 'I'll go. No point in all of us getting out in the freezing cold.'

'I'm so glad you said that.' Christy wrapped her long, heavy cardigan across her body even though she couldn't possibly be cold. The heating was on and set to a balmy twenty-three degrees.

Cathy stepped out and sucked in her breath. It was absolutely freezing. She dashed to the boot, yanked out her coat and gloves and, wrapping her scarf around her neck, quickly put them on, stepping from foot to foot to try to keep the circulation going in her legs while she rummaged for her handbag. It hadn't felt anywhere near as bitter as this when they'd left Milton Keynes this morning, or when they'd stopped halfway to have the breakfast they missed by leaving so early.

She jumped up and down in front of the car to show Christy just how cold she was before dashing up the icy path, slipping and sliding as she did so. She reached the door and rang the bell. She rang it again after a couple of minutes. And again, a minute or two later.

'Okay, okay. Where's the fire?' someone shouted from inside.

Oh dear. This wasn't a very good start.

The door sprung open and a dishevelled-looking woman about Cathy's age stood yawning before her.

'This had better be good,' the woman said. 'It's only just nine and choir practice adjourned to the pub. Oh. Who are you?' The woman's perfectly shaped, blonde brows met, and cool blue-green eyes looked Cathy up and down.

'Good morning. Sorry. We wanted to get here before the blizzard they forecast for today arrives and I thought … It doesn't matter. Um. I'm Cathy Cole. My friend and I are renting Corner Cottage for the holidays.' She gave her friendliest smile and kept her fingers crossed behind her back. So many things had gone wrong lately. She couldn't bear another disappointment.

'Cathy? Oh yes. Cathy. Come in, come in. It's freezing out there. Sorry. Forgive me snapping. Had a few too many wines last night and didn't get to bed until two a.m. because we were Googling reindeer and sleighs. But you don't want to know about that.' She stepped aside to let Cathy pass. 'I'm Ella. Oh God. And this gorgeous hunk coming down the stairs in just his jeans is my boyfriend, Gill. Would you like a cup of coffee, Cathy? Gill will be making a pot as soon as he gets dressed.' She grinned and shook her head.

Cathy hadn't noticed the man nearing the foot of the stairs, but now that Ella had pointed him out, Cathy silently agreed with her. He was a gorgeous hunk. Tall, broad, with wavy chestnut brown hair, expensive-looking glasses that made him more handsome, not less (she could spot a designer frame a mile away) and a six-pack any woman would like to run her hands over.

'Hello. I'm pleased to meet you both. I won't stay for coffee, if you don't mind. My friend and our kids are in the car. I just need the key please, and to pay you. I assume we should pay in advance and then settle up for extras at the end of the holiday? I'd rather not use a credit card, if that's okay with you. I've got plenty of cash and I'm happy to leave some now to go towards the extras.'

Ella yawned again. 'Extras? Um. What extras are you expecting?' She glanced anxiously towards her boyfriend.

Cathy smiled. 'I meant for things like the electricity and gas we use. Those are often billed at the end of the holiday.' Not that she knew that for certain because this was the first rental holiday she had ever been on, but she'd read that on the internet, so assumed it must be true. 'And for any damage caused. Not that there'll be any, I promise. Christy and I are careful and our kids are well-behaved.'

'Are they? The extras, I'm talking about. Not your kids' behaviour.' Ella smiled, but again she glanced at Gill, who shrugged and made his way along the hall.

'Call Mia,' he said. 'She'll be up because Jet will have got up with the lark, as always, and they'll already have had breakfast.'

'Good idea,' Ella said. 'It's not my cottage, you see. It belongs to my best friend, Mia Ward. She's at her boyfriend's house. Again.'

Cathy glanced over her shoulder at the closed front door. 'Is it possible for me to pay you, sign something, and leave extra, then sort it out later, please? My daughter's six and she doesn't like being away from me for longer than five minutes, at the moment, so she'll start getting anxious and possibly crying, any second. Not that there's anything wrong. It's just that … we've been through some big changes over the last couple of

102

years and she hasn't coped that well with the most recent ones. Changes at home are unsettling for children. Sorry, now I'm rambling.'

'No. It's my fault,' Ella said, with a friendly smile. 'We've been through a few changes here, so I know how unsettling they can be, for adults, let alone children. My brother was dating Mia but his ex-girlfriend … God! Listen to me going on. There's plenty of time for us all to get to know one another. I'll get the key. I know Mia printed out an invoice and that'll probably be with the key. Gill? Is there an invoice with the key to Corner Cottage? It'll be near the wine rack. The key's on the hook above it.'

'Yeah,' Gill called after a moment's silence, before appearing in the hall, key in one hand, invoice in the other and handed them to Ella, who glanced at the invoice and passed it to Cathy.

Cathy took her purse from her bag and counted out the notes to pay in full, adding another one hundred pounds for the extras. It shouldn't come to that, but she'd rather pay more, in the hope that this Mia woman wouldn't insist on taking her credit card details. She didn't want to use her credit cards. He could trace those. And that meant he would find them. Which was something she wanted to avoid at any cost.

Chapter Fourteen

'If I'd known they were arriving early this morning I would have made sure I had been here,' Mia said when Ella informed her of Cathy and Christy's arrival, not more than fifteen minutes after Cathy had left.

'I tried to call you, but Jet said you'd already left. Did you walk here? It's freezing out there. Why didn't Jet give you a lift?'

Mia grinned. 'You're right. It is freezing. I don't suppose there's any coffee, is there?'

'I'll make some fresh,' Gill offered.

'To answer your other questions,' Mia continued, pulling out a kitchen chair and sitting at the table. 'Jet offered to bring me, obviously, but I wanted to walk. Even though it's bitterly cold, it's such a lovely morning. The snow was so crisp, pristine and sparkly, and it was unbelievably peaceful this morning. I simply wanted to take it all in. The foxes' footprints across the fields.

Plump robins feasting on holly berries. The seagulls soaring across the sky which was almost ice blue, with merely a puff or two of fluffy white clouds. It was beautiful.'

Ella gave her an odd look. 'Meanwhile, back on planet Earth.' She grinned. 'Cathy didn't want to use a credit card, which is probably just as well because I don't think you have the facility to take them, do you?'

Mia shook her head. 'That didn't even occur to me. The Hardmans paid their money directly to my bank.'

'Nor me. Anyway, she wanted to pay cash. Which she did. And she also paid another one hundred pounds for extras.'

'Extras? What extras?'

Ella laughed. 'That's exactly what I said. Apparently, when people rent holiday cottages they pay for things like electricity, gas, and breakages at the end of their stay. I gave her the key, and Gill, who was half naked at the time...' She rolled her eyes. '... Don't ask. Anyway, Gill explained how the Aga and the heating worked. He also reminded her that there was no TV and no mobile reception, but that there was a landline and also reasonable broadband. She seemed pretty happy. And I think she really liked the decorations. She said both she and her friend were astonished that we'd put them up. You see. I told you they'd like the snowmen and the candy canes.'

Mia grinned. 'Are you sure that's what she meant by "astonished"? Thanks for explaining all that, Gill. I'll pop in and say hello later this morning, once they've settled in. At least, if we do get the blizzard predicted for today, they won't have to worry about getting to the shops. The welcome pack of food we left should cover the essentials for a day or two.'

Gill handed Mia a cup of coffee. 'I reminded her that the shops were a good fifteen miles away, and explained about the welcome pack, but she said they'd brought quite a few things with them. Although she needs to get all the food for Christmas dinner, and stuff like that. I also told her about Lake's Bakes, and that she could get milk, butter, eggs and cheese from Little Pond Farm.'

'Well, I don't think I need to do anything then, do I? Other than say hello and give her Jet's landline number in case of emergencies. And I'll mention the charity carol evening, too, in case they want to come along to that. How old were the kids?'

Ella shrugged. 'No idea. They were in the car with her friend.'

'Didn't you go out and say hello?'

Ella raised her brows. 'Are you mad? It's bloody freezing out there? I'm not setting foot outside this cottage today. Not for anything or anyone. Besides, we need to do some packing today because you know what this means, don't you?'

Mia beamed at her and nodded. 'Yep. It means I'm moving in with Jet.'

'*We're* moving in with Jet,' Ella corrected. 'And it's only for the holidays, don't forget.'

Mia let her shoulders slump dramatically before grinning broadly and sitting up straight. 'Unless I continue renting out Corner Cottage, and you continue making mistakes and double booking.' She winked at Ella and grinned at Gill. 'Or do you think that might be pushing my luck?'

Ella took the coffee Gill handed her and gave a little frown. 'Do you want to push your luck? Are you saying you would actually like to move in with him? Are you ready for that? And more importantly, do you honestly think he's ready for that? This is the man who, only a few months ago, swore he would never ask any woman to move in with him. Although that was before he realised he was madly in love with you, of course. But even so, that's one hell of a step, Mia.'

Mia shrugged. 'I know it is. And to be completely honest, I don't know if either of us is really ready for such a major step. But the thing is, we haven't spent one night apart since Halloween. Either he's here, or I'm at his place, so we are almost as good as living together now. And I really loved the supper party and decorating the house for Christmas. It simply felt so right. I'm joking though. I wouldn't really try to trick him into letting me stay.'

'Letting us stay, you mean.' Ella nudged her arm. 'You keep forgetting me and Gill.'

'How could I possibly do that?' Mia pulled a face and laughed.

Gill sat at the table and cradled his coffee, a serious expression on his face. 'I think you need to see how these two weeks go before you make any long-term plans. Christmas can be hell for relationships.'

Mia and Ella looked at one another, then glared at him.

'Thanks for that, Gill,' Ella said. 'Nothing like a positive outlook to make the festive season bright.' She shook her head and sipped her coffee.

'And on that cheerful note,' Mia added, letting out a little sigh. 'I'd better phone Jet and give him the good news.'

Chapter Fifteen

In spite of the bitter cold, or possibly because of it, it didn't take more than a few hours to move Mia, Ella and Gill's belongings to Little Pond Farm. Jet said it needed to be done that day and during daylight hours because Thursday was rugby practice and in any event Mia and Ella together with Hettie, wanted to spend all day Thursday preparing Sunbeam Cottage for the Hardman's arrival. That meant Mia, Ella and Gill only had Wednesday morning in which to pack, but Lori came over and helped, so even that didn't take as long as Mia had expected.

'Don't forget the rowing machine in the dining room,' Mia reminded them as Jet, Gill and Franklin carried the last of the boxes to Jet's battered old Land Rover and the spacious trailer attached. It was just as well he had those, because none of their belongings would fit into his new car and they would never be able to hire a van at such short notice. Even if they had used Mia's car and Gill's and Franklin's, it would've taken far, far longer.

Jet rolled his eyes and shook his head. 'Have you ever used that thing?'

'Yes,' Mia said, indignantly. 'I just can't remember when.'

'Then it's going in the cellar.'

'Fine.'

The truth was, Mia had always meant to use it, but somehow she just didn't seem to get around to it. It was a bit like two years ago when she had paid a fortune for gym membership, but never went to the gym. Last year she had bought the rowing machine to save herself the expensive fee, and the hassle of going out in the cold to get to the gym. But since she had been in Little Pondale, she got quite enough exercise without it. Swimming, running, kite flying and all the other activities she, Ella and Lori had participated in – not to mention all the sex the three of them had had this year – helped to keep them all in better shape than they had ever been in London.

Or perhaps, in Mia and Ella's case, it was because they were eating far more healthily these days. Garrick and Lori had cooked for them, save for the few weeks after Garrick left, when Lori moved in with Franklin, and they reverted to their old ways of cooking frozen pizza or various ding dinners before Gill arrived in October. They hadn't had a ready meal or frozen pizza since.

And that had been on Mia's mind rather more than usual recently. She had never really learnt to cook and nor had Ella. When Mia had lived at home, Lori had cooked every meal. Lori hated messy kitchens and the moment Mia stepped into one, more often than not, it would look as if a troop of monkeys had tried to prepare a meal. Living in her bijou, rented flat in London meant the kitchen was tiny, and it was far easier to eat out. Once, she had tried to cook a four-course meal to impress a particular boyfriend, but three courses were inedible and even the salad starter was limp.

It had already been decided that Gill would be cooking Christmas dinner, but Mia had started wondering if, perhaps, it was time to work on her kitchen skills. Wouldn't it be wonderful to place the golden bronzed, basted turkey in front of Jet to carve, and to be able to say that she had prepared it with her own hands? Well, that she had put it in the oven, set the correct temperature, and cooked it for the required amount of time to ensure it sliced to perfection and melted in the mouth.

But she didn't have time to worry about that right now. She needed to get her things to Jet's and get them all unpacked.

'Is there any chance we could drop in at Corner Cottage before we head to yours?' she asked, as Jet and Gill carried the rowing machine to the trailer. 'I wanted to say hello to Cathy and her friend and to give her your landline number in case of emergencies. Is that okay?'

Jet shoved the rowing machine in place and tied sturdy straps around it to make sure it didn't fall off. 'No problem. Do you want me to come too?'

'I think it might be nice if you just said hello.'

'We could all say hello,' Lori said. 'Show them some friendly faces and let them know who's who, and what's what.'

Mia grinned at her. 'Rather than let Hettie tell them, you mean?'

Lori shrugged. 'It did cross my mind.'

Less than five minutes later, Mia rang the bell at Corner Cottage.

After an anxious sounding, 'Who is it?' from a female voice within, the door was opened by a woman who looked a similar age to Mia, with long, shiny hair the colour of melted toffee, pale skin drawn tightly over high cheekbones and possibly the palest blue eyes Mia had ever seen, but currently filled with concern.

'Hello,' Mia said. 'I'm Mia and this is my boyfriend Jet, my mum, Lori and her partner, Franklin. Ella and Gill you've already met. Sorry to disturb you but we just wanted to introduce ourselves and I wanted to give you a new contact number in case you need anything, or in the event of an emergency. We're going to be staying at Little Pond Farm from today, and another party will be renting Sunbeam Cottage.'

'Oh, hi. I'm Cathy. Pleased to meet you all. Thanks for this,' she said, as everyone welcomed her, and Mia handed her a sheet of paper.

'It gives you the new phone number, my email address and the address of Little Pond Farm, together with directions of how to get there. I believe Gill's already told you that the farm sells milk, butter, eggs and cheese, and take it from me, you've never tasted cheese like it.'

'She means it's good, I hope,' Jet said, smiling.

'You know I do. That's why I love you. It's for your cheese.'

'Oh? Not my abundance of charm, my wonderful sense of humour, good looks and fabulous personality then?' He raised an eyebrow in mock indignation.

'Those too.' Mia grinned at him before turning her attention back to Cathy. 'Ella's very kindly drawn you a little map of the village, showing Lake's Bakes, where you'll get the most delicious bread, cakes and other baked delights. That's Rupert's cottage,' she said, pointing at the map. 'He's the local vet but he's also a first responder slash paramedic, so he's the man to go to if you have an accident. Which I'm sure you won't, but it's good to know he's there. We all call him Bear. The vicar's cottage is marked with the word 'vicarage' beside it. His name's Glen and he's fairly new to the village. This is his third week, I believe. There are arrows pointing to the top of the church steeple and also to the top of Frog Hill. They're the only places for mobile reception, but there's broadband, so you can keep in touch via email and although there's no TV, you can stream stuff if you've got suitable devices. And finally, it shows The Frog and Lily. Ella's helpfully written the word, 'pub' beside that, in case you're in any doubt.' She threw Ella a grin. 'I think that's everything you need to know, but please don't hesitate to ask if you have any questions. I hope you're settling in and that you have a lovely stay.'

Cathy scanned the sheet of paper and smiled. 'Thanks again. I think this covers everything. The cottage is beautiful and so is the village. It's exactly what we hoped it would be. I'm sure we're going to have a wonderful time. I apologise for arriving early this morning but we wanted to get here before the blizzard they forecast. Not that's it's arrived.'

'No need to apologise. We're usually early risers. Well. We'd better leave you to it.'

'What about the carol evening?' Lori asked. 'Weren't you going to mention that, darling?'

'Oh yes. Thanks, Mum. I don't know if you and your friend are interested but on Saturday night the choir and some others from the village will be going to every house, singing carols for charity. There's a buffet in the pub afterwards. Most people will be there and you're welcome to come along and join us. Don't feel you have to though, if you'd rather not, but you'll find this is a very friendly, welcoming place. Ella, Mum and I only moved here this spring, and we already feel like locals. So does Gill, and he only arrived in October.'

'That sounds great,' Cathy said. 'I'll mention it to Christy. Sorry. She's giving the kids a bath at the moment. The minute they saw this cottage backs onto a beach, they were on the sand, even though most of it's still got a cover of snow. Needless to say, they got very cold and wet. But they loved it, and that's all that matters.'

Mia was certain she saw sadness in Cathy's eyes, even though the woman was laughing.

'Children do love to play on a beach,' Lori said. 'How old are they?'

'My daughter, Daisy is six and Dylan, Christy's daughter is four.'

'Do they still believe in Father Christmas?' Gill asked, and Ella gave him a very odd look.

Cathy stiffened visibly. 'Dylan does. Daisy was told by … someone recently that he didn't exist, but Christy and I have told her that he does exist, if a person wants him to. If that makes sense.'

'It makes perfect sense,' Mia said, beaming. 'I believe in him and so does Ella.' She winked. 'And perhaps I shouldn't say this, because it's not definite yet, but we may be getting some genuine reindeer for Little Pond Farm, for Christmas. And possibly a sleigh. We'll let you know how it goes.'

'Reindeer? And a sleigh? Wow. The kids would love that.'

The sun suddenly disappeared behind a bank of clouds and large, white flakes fell from the sky.

'And here comes the snow again,' Ella said, her excitement evident for all to see as she held out her hands to catch the massive snowflakes.

'We'd better get going,' Jet said, as a gust of wind sent the snowflakes spiralling. 'I think that blizzard may be on the way. Don't forget where we are if you need anything.'

They all hurriedly said goodbye and dashed towards their vehicles, but Lori grabbed Mia's hand and pulled her close as Cathy closed the front door.

'I may be wrong, darling,' she whispered. 'And anything could have caused it, but unless I am very much mistaken, Cathy had the remnants of what was once a black eye. And did you see how anxious she looked?'

'A black eye? I didn't see that, but she did look a little worried, I agree with you on that score. And extremely pale. Although if you're right about the eye, perhaps that was make-up. God, Mum. Are you saying you think she may have been the victim of some sort of domestic abuse? I'm sure Ella told me that Cathy said there had been some big changes at her home recently. Perhaps she's left her husband.'

Lori shrugged. 'I may be jumping to conclusions, but I've seen that look before.'

Chapter Sixteen

The forecasted blizzard arrived. Mia and the others had just enough time to get everything inside the farmhouse before it set in with a vengeance. The wind was verging on gale force and outside, the candy canes and Norway Spruce bent at precarious angles and myriad lights swayed wildly to and fro. The snow was so heavy that Mia could not see as far as the wooden gate halfway down the drive, and the Georgian windows rattled and moaned against the onslaught. Little M lay curled up in her bed beside the fire but every now and then she raised her head and barked, her large brown eyes darting towards Mia as if the dog was saying, 'I'm okay if you're okay, but if you move, I'm outta here.'

'I've never seen snow like this,' Mia said, huddled between Ella and Lori on one of two large sofas in the sitting room, this one facing towards the double set of front windows, with the fireplace to her right.

A roaring fire crackled beneath the evergreen-covered marble mantelpiece, as wind whistled down the chimney, making the flames dance and sputter in the hearth.

'Neither have I,' said Lori, cradling a mug of steaming hot chocolate. 'It was kind of Jet to suggest we stay here until this storm abates. I know our farm cottage is less than a mile away, but I'm not sure we would find it in this weather.'

'I hope the snowmen and reindeer don't get blown off the roofs of the cottages,' said Ella. 'Imagine the damage they could do if they hit someone on the head. Although I suppose it would give the kids in Corner Cottage a bit of a thrill to see flying reindeer, even if Father Christmas was nowhere in sight.' She grinned and blew on her hot chocolate.

'I just hope we don't see flying men,' Mia added. 'Do you think we should go and see if they're all okay?'

Gill and Franklin had remained outside helping Jet and Pete secure the barn doors and anything that might take flight in such strong winds, but they'd been out there for over twenty minutes, and Mia was beginning to get a little worried, especially as it was getting dark. At this time of year it was dark at half past four, but because of the blizzard it seemed to be darker even earlier today.

'Perhaps we should,' Ella agreed, but no one made a move.

'I'm sure they're fine,' Lori said, the wind howling so loud that it almost made Mia jump.

A crash, followed by a bang did make her jump. It also made Little M bark, leap up and dash towards the sofa.

'That's it.' Mia leant forward, put her mug on the coffee table, stroked Little M's head and got to her feet. 'I've got to go and see if they need help.'

Ella sighed and did the same. 'Must we?' She gave Mia a pleading look.

'I think we must,' Lori said, following Mia's lead.

Luckily, at that precise moment Jet, Gill and Franklin appeared in the doorway and Little M raced towards Jet, madly wagging her tail.

'We were just coming to see if we could help,' Mia said, walking over to Jet.

He shook his head. 'It's best you don't go out in that. It's pretty serious stuff out there. I'm not sure if this is a blizzard or a hurricane. The last time we had weather like this, I think I was a kid. We lost half the tiles from the church steeple roof as well as a couple of thatched roofs of the cottages on Frog Hill. I hope your visitors are okay.'

'I think they would call if they're not,' Mia said. 'Come and sit down all of you and we'll go and make you something hot to drink. Oh. Where's Pete?' She looked anxiously at Jet, who smiled.

'Don't worry. He hasn't been blown away. At least I hope he hasn't. I told him he could stay, but he wanted to get home and be with his wife, so I let him go before it got worse. He left about fifteen minutes ago and should be home by now. I asked him to give me a quick ring and let me know.'

The landline rang as Jet was finishing his sentence and he grinned and picked up the phone from the table nearby.

'Hi, Pete ... Really? ... Thanks for letting me know.' He hung up, frowning. 'Some of the fences are down and Pete says there're already massive banks of snow on Seaside Road. If this continues, no one's going anywhere for the rest of today and tonight. Hopefully, the council will get the snowploughs out tomorrow, but I wouldn't count on that. I've got a plough we can attach to one of the tractors, so at least I can clear the yard, the drive and the exit onto Seaside Road, but other than that...' He shrugged and let his voice trail off. Finally, he smiled, slid an arm around Mia's waist and pulled her to him. 'What a good thing we moved you in this afternoon. A few more hours and we might not have been able to get you here.'

'Perfect timing,' she said, smiling up at him as he kissed her quickly on the lips.

'It looks like you and Franklin will be staying the night, Lori,' Jet continued. 'I'll get a bed made up.'

'We'll do that,' Mia said. 'You sit down and relax. You've had a busy day.'

Jet laughed. 'This wasn't a busy day. It was an unusual day for a farmer, but it wasn't busy, except perhaps for the last half an hour. But if you're sure. Making beds isn't on my list of favourite pastimes. A bed needs to be made up for Ella and Gill, too. I haven't done that yet. Everything you need is either in the airing cupboard at the top of the first flight of stairs and to your left, or in the linen cupboard in the utility room. Help yourself to anything.' He glanced at Gill and Franklin. 'I think we deserve half an hour beside the fire. As for those hot drinks, Mia. Personally, I'd prefer a large brandy, and one of Hettie's mince pies, if there are any left.'

'Same here, please' said Gill, dashing towards the fire and giving Ella a quick kiss on the way.

'Sounds good,' Franklin said, hugging Lori.

'I'll go and get them.' Mia eased herself out of Jet's arms and headed towards the kitchen.

'We'll make the beds,' Lori said, grabbing Ella by the arm and pulling her towards the door.

'Must we?' Ella whined, but she was grinning. 'I'd much rather stay beside the fire.'

'You can do that later,' Mia told her. 'There won't be anything else to do if it's as bad out there as Pete said, so it'll be an evening by the fire for us all.'

'Not necessarily,' said Jet, winking and grinning devilishly. 'I can think of other ways to spend the evening.'

Mia grinned back. 'What? Like playing charades, you mean? Ella, Mum and I love charades, don't we?' She winked at them.

Jet laughed. 'Of course, my beautiful, sexy girlfriend. Charades was precisely what I had in mind.'

The blizzard eventually blew itself out around midnight and, despite Mia's joke, they had in fact all spent the evening playing charades. And not just charades. They played Monopoly, Poker – which Ella suggested should be strip poker, but Jet said there was no way he was losing his clothes in front of his girlfriend's mum, and Snap. How they went from poker to Snap, no one was quite sure, but Mia said it must have had something to do with the amount of wine and brandy they had been drinking.

Gill made chilli con carne for supper, and Mia had asked if she could help, so needless to say, the kitchen now looked as if a troop of drunken monkeys, not just monkeys, had been in there.

Rod Stewart's Christmas Album had played in the background. It had been Sarah Cross' favourite, and Jet said he always played it at this time of year. Lori had been impressed. Rod Stewart was one of her favourite's too. Even Mia had enjoyed it, although she'd been equally pleased when Jet had put on a selection of other Christmas songs.

The indoor lights twinkled and sparkled, the house was cosy and warm, and everyone forgot about the blizzard – until the following morning.

'God, it's bitter out there,' Jet said, shaking off a covering of snowflakes and rubbing his gloved hands together as he came into the kitchen from the farmyard with Little M at his heels. 'Oh. What happened in here?'

'I happened,' Mia said, pouring him a large mug of coffee. He'd gone straight out after showering earlier, telling Mia he wanted to check on the chickens and cows, so he hadn't stopped for coffee, and he'd used the front door so that he could briefly inspect the outdoor decorations.

He laughed. 'Do you always make this much mess when you cook? It's never looked like this before when you've stayed.'

'That's because I've never cooked before. You have. Or we've eaten out. And yes, I do always make this much mess. That's one of the reasons I don't cook. But all that's going to change. I'm going to learn to do things properly, and Mum and Gill have promised to teach me – and be patient while they do so. Right now, I'm going to make you eggs on toast. Just as soon as I can find the toaster. And the eggs. And the pan. Do you know what any of those things look like?' she joked.

He grinned as he walked over and kissed her. He pointed to the large four-slice toaster on the worktop. 'I think that's the thing you cook the eggs in. But you'd better check with Lori first because I could be wrong.'

She gave him a playful slap. 'You're a good cook, like Gill, so you may laugh, but wait until Christmas Day. I'm determined I'm going to prepare Christmas dinner with my own fair hands. It'll be the best turkey you've ever tasted.'

'Excellent,' he said, taking the coffee she gave him and gulping a mouthful down. 'Do you know how to pluck a turkey?'

A shiver ran through her. 'Er. Pluck it? Don't they all come without feathers?'

'They do if you buy one from the shops. Not if you get one from the local, free-range turkey farmer. They come fresh from the field.' He grinned again. 'Don't look so horrified. He also sells them ready-plucked. I was teasing you.'

'Well don't. My heart almost stopped when you said "pluck".'

'Don't use *fowl* language this early in the morning,' Ella said, joining them and smiling at her own joke. 'God. What happened in here?'

'Don't you start,' said Mia, pouring her a coffee. 'I should've cleared up last night like Gill said we should, but we could hardly stand by the time we went to bed.'

'Morning.' Lori followed behind Ella. 'Shall I make breakfast for us all, darling? If that's all right with you, of course, Jet?'

'Make yourself at home,' Jet said, smiling at her.

'I'd better clear up first, Mum.' Mia grabbed some of the pans and took them to the dishwasher.

'We can do that later,' Lori said. 'I don't think you'll be going anywhere today. Have you looked outside?'

'At least the blizzard's stopped,' Jet said. 'But it's cold out there and it's still snowing. The best place for everyone today is indoors. Unless, like me and Franklin, they've got a farm to run.'

Mia handed Lori a cup of coffee and turned her attention back to Jet. 'I've got to get this place looking like a kitchen again and not a war zone and Mum, Ella and I are going to Sunbeam Cottage today to do some clearing up in preparation for the Hardman's arrival tomorrow. Assuming they can get here through this snow. But once we've done that, I can help around the farm.'

He raised his brows. 'With the chickens and cows?'

She nodded. 'Now's as good a time to start as any.'

He beamed at her. 'Did you fall over and hit your head without me realising? Determined to learn to cook? Willing to risk being eaten alive by a chicken or a cow? Are you sure?'

'Very funny. Yes. I'm sure.'

He nodded. 'Okay then. I think I'm going to like having you living here. And that's something I never thought I'd hear myself say about a woman.'

'Ah,' Ella said. 'But Mia's not just any woman, is she?'

Jet stared at Mia over the rim of his coffee mug. 'No. You can say that again. She definitely isn't.'

And although Mia wasn't one hundred per cent sure what he meant by that comment, from the look he was giving her, it sounded like something good. Something very, very good.

Chapter Seventeen

Cathy stiffened, staring at the ringing telephone. The first ring made her jump. The second sent a cold, unpleasant trickle of anxiety through her veins. The third made her give herself a reality check. It couldn't be him. He couldn't know they were here.

'Are you going to answer that?' Christy called out from the kitchen. 'It might be Mia to see if we survived the blizzard.' She popped her head around the doorway. 'Do you want me to get it?'

Cathy shook her head. 'No, I'll be fine. You're right. It won't be him. It can't be.' Gingerly, she picked up the receiver. 'Hello?'

'Morning. It's Mia. Is that Cathy?'

Cathy breathed a sigh of relief. 'Morning, Mia. Yes, it is. How are you?'

'Fine thanks, but more importantly, how are you? Did the cottage survive the onslaught?' There was a hint of laughter in Mia's voice, but it was obvious that she was genuinely concerned.

'No signs of damage as far as we can see,' Cathy said. 'Christy and I briefly nipped outside when we got up and the snowman on the roof looks a little drunk and the candy canes are all leaning to the left – but aren't we all?' She gave a little laugh. 'Other than that, everything looked fine. Daisy and Dylan are still fast asleep because they didn't get much sleep last night. Neither of them is used to the sounds old houses make and on top of that and the wind, Christy and I sat up with them past midnight.'

'Oh, I'm so sorry Cathy.' Mia sounded sincere.

Cathy smiled down the phone and cheerfully replied, 'It's not your fault, Mia. They forecasted the blizzard, so we should have been prepared. The minute the kids see how much snow there is outside this morning, last night will quickly be forgotten. And the cottage was so warm and cosy, especially with the roaring log fire. It may sound weird, but neither of the children has seen a real fire before, and they were fascinated by it. A couple of our friends have wood-burning stoves but they're not quite the same as an open fire in a hearth, are they? And that massive fireguard that locks into position meant they were perfectly safe.'

'It looks as though it may brighten up later,' Mia said. 'The forecast is for snow this morning but sunshine this afternoon, so hopefully your children will be able to build snowmen later.'

Cathy laughed. 'They'll be out there building snowmen the minute they finish breakfast, snow or not. Oh, and from the squeals of delight I've just heard from upstairs, I think I can say they're up and have looked out of the window.'

'I'd better let you go then,' Mia said. 'Don't forget to call us if you need anything. Have a lovely day.'

'Thanks. And you.' Cathy hung up the phone, smiled at Christy who was loitering in the hall, and ran up the stairs to the children's rooms.

'It's snowing, Mummy.' Daisy was kneeling on the window seat in her bedroom, with Dylan, who was shorter, standing beside her. Both of them were beaming as they peered through the window as if it were a doorway to paradise.

'There's lots of snow on the floor,' Dylan said, briefly glancing over her shoulder, eyes as wide as saucers.

'Lots of snow on the ground,' Cathy corrected, smiling. 'Why don't we get you both dressed and then, once you've had breakfast, we can all go outside and build snowmen, make snow angels and maybe throw a couple of little snowballs at your Mummy, Dylan.'

Dylan turned round again, her little mouth forming a perfect 'O' and her eyes alight with glee. She clapped her tiny hands together and her blonde curls bounced up and down as she did.

Christy, who had come upstairs to join them, tutted at Dylan. 'Don't jump up and down on someone else's furniture, darling. We're not at home now.' She playfully nudged Cathy out of the way and, dashing towards the window, she grabbed Dylan, lifted her high in the air and swung her round and round in a circle.

Dylan giggled and shrieked. 'Stop Mummy. Stop.' But when Christy did stop, Dylan looked disappointed and said, 'More Mummy. More.'

'Once more and then we've got to get you dressed.'

Cathy picked Daisy up and swung her in a half circle. 'Oh. You're such a big girl. Too grown-up for me to swing you round.' She beamed at her daughter and gave her a big, sloppy kiss. 'But not too big for me to eat you all up.'

Daisy laughed and pushed her hands against Cathy's shoulders. 'You're silly, Mummy.'

'I know.' Cathy put Daisy on the floor and crouched down to be at eye level. 'But you love me lots.'

She hugged Daisy tightly and Daisy threw her arms around Cathy's neck.

'Lots and lots, Mummy.'

Cathy closed her eyes and kissed Daisy's toffee-coloured locks, which were long and straight like her own hair. She hugged Daisy tightly and a lump formed in her throat. This was going to be their best Christmas for some time. She was going to make sure of that.

They had struggled financially over the last three years, and more so during the past few months. Cathy's parents had died when she was in her twenties, but when she married, she had been financially secure. She thought she'd be that way for life, but things can change in the blink of an eye, and they had certainly changed for Cathy.

Cathy's grandad had often helped her out, although she had never told him quite how bad things were. When he died, two months ago, he left her several thousand pounds, which she had eventually received last month after sorting out his will herself. He hadn't owned his own house, and his savings weren't enough to make her rich, but they were enough to change her and Daisy's lives for the better.

That was how they could afford this holiday, and paying for Christy and Dylan to come with them, had been Cathy's gift to her best friend. She had used some of the money to pay her debts and current bills and to finally clear her credit cards. She'd got herself a cheap, fairly old used car so that she had more freedom to get around and had also bought a few new clothes for Daisy.

But the best thing was, she had bought several of the gifts she knew her daughter wanted but didn't expect to get. Daisy might be young but she knew that they were poor. Cathy couldn't wait for Christmas morning to see Daisy's face light up. She hadn't gone overboard. Cathy had never been extravagant in her life, but Daisy deserved a few treats. She'd been through so much. They both had.

But perhaps the Christmas presents weren't the best things to come out of her grandad's money. Perhaps this holiday was. The fact that Daisy was going to be able to do all the things a child of her age should, and Cathy was going to do them with her, without feeling anxious every time the doorbell or the phone rang (although clearly that might take a day or two to get used to) and without having someone watching them, or turning up uninvited and then criticising Cathy's every move. And not just hers, but Daisy's too. The money gave her freedom. It gave them both a chance to start their lives anew.

'Come on you,' Christy said, tapping Cathy playfully on the arm. 'Let's get these two dressed and fed so that we can all go outside and have some fun.'

Cathy opened her eyes and smiled up at her friend, nodding as she did so. 'Fun. Absolutely. Lots and lots of fun.'

And less than half an hour later they were doing precisely that.

It was still snowing, but the flakes were falling slowly and steadily without so much as a breath of wind to blow them off their downward trajectory. After the winds of last night, it was almost eerily quiet in the village this morning.

Being at the end of Lily Pond Lane, or start, depending on which way you looked at it, the front garden of Corner Cottage afforded a view all the way up the lane towards the pond, the pub and the church. No doubt in summer, this village could win any of the 'Prettiest Village in the UK' competitions; even now, covered in snow, the village was stunningly beautiful.

Yesterday, before the blizzard had started, Cathy looked out of the sitting room window across at the ice-covered pond glistening in the warm yellow lights from the lampposts. Strings of multi-coloured lights swayed gently between them, casting rainbow-like reflections on the snow and oddly enough, Cathy had felt at home.

But this was like no home she had ever lived in. She lived in Milton Keynes, or had until now, and that was about as opposite to this village in every way it was possible to be. If there were any thatched cottages in Milton Keynes, she hadn't seen them, and on the estate where she lived, an empty lane without another person in sight, was unheard of. Her street had been full of children riding bikes, kicking balls or playing tag, and adults chatting, walking their dogs, fixing their cars or tending to their tiny gardens.

Those things probably happened here too, but on a much, much smaller scale. And this morning, when she had woken up, once she had remembered where she was, she had lain in bed revelling in the silence which was broken only by the occasional burst of birdsong. As bizarre as it might seem, she felt as if her very soul was being healed. Even

Christy had commented on how incredibly quiet it was first thing this morning when Cathy had taken her a cup of coffee at eight o'clock, and how lovely it was not to be woken by revving engines, blaring car horns, or hordes of noisy neighbours.

'I could get used to this,' Christy had said.

'So could I,' Cathy had replied.

And now, watching Daisy showing Dylan how to make snow angels, laughing and happy as a six-year-old should be, Cathy made a decision. She couldn't afford to live in a place like Little Pondale, obviously, but perhaps there were some flats or smaller houses in one of the nearby villages, or the town fifteen miles or so away, that she could rent. Granted, she had only been away from Milton Keynes for twenty-four hours, but in her heart she already knew she didn't want to return. She didn't know how Christy would feel about it, and Cathy would miss her best friend dreadfully, but other than Christy, now that her grandad had gone, there was nothing and no one to keep her in Milton Keynes. But there was someone she definitely wanted to get away from.

'Good morning.' A male voice behind her said, momentarily making her heart skip a beat until she realised she didn't recognise it. 'They look as though they're having fun. My name's Glen and I'm the vicar at St Michael and All Angels. Well, temporary vicar. How are you settling in? I hope the blizzard didn't terrify you.'

Cathy turned to face him and was surprised at how young and handsome he was. For some reason she had assumed the vicar in a village like this would be old, with wispy grey hair, glasses perched on the end of his nose, and a welcoming, friendly smile, like her grandad had been. Not that he had been a vicar. But whenever she thought of elderly, friendly men, she saw her grandad's face. She missed him so much. When he died, it broke her heart all over again, even though the cancer had been killing him for years and now he was finally free from pain.

'Good morning, Reverend,' she said, smiling. 'It did keep us awake until the early hours, but once we fell asleep, we slept like logs. As for settling in, we already feel at home, thank you, and yes, Daisy and Dylan here, are having a wonderful time.'

'Why temporary?' Christy asked. She had been inside making mugs of hot chocolate for the four of them and must have been on her way out again as the vicar was speaking.

Cathy raised her brows, also curious about that.

'Let's just say that the former incumbent had to leave in rather a hurry,' Glen said, smiling oddly.

'That sounds intriguing,' Cathy said, the warmth of Glen's smile making her feel even more at home.

'You'll no doubt hear all about it.' He shook his head but he was smiling. 'But not from me. So, is it just the four of you? And more importantly, do you like carol singing?'

'It's just the four of us,' Christy replied. 'And before we answer that, perhaps we'd better ask why?' She winked at him and smiled.

Cathy tutted quietly. 'You shouldn't wink at a vicar, Christy. It's not polite.'

Glen laughed. 'You can wink at this vicar as much as you like. I don't mind at all. The only reason I asked was because we're having a carol singing charity evening on Saturday and I wondered if you'd like to join in.'

Cathy and Christy glanced at one another and smiled. 'Mia and her friends have already told us about that. And yes, we'd love to. Although we're not sure the children will last for very long. And they're usually in bed by seven, or eight at the latest.'

Glen nodded. 'Of course. Why would they want to stand around in the snow when they could be playing in it instead? Or curled up fast asleep in their beds. Both of which I'd rather be doing, to be honest. But as I'm the vicar, I suppose I should make some effort. No doubt Mia has told you about Lake's Bakes. Jenny, who runs the bakery, makes the most delicious bread and cakes in the country, I'm sure, and she's a lovely person too.'

'Yes,' Cathy said, grinning. The locals certainly liked to promote the businesses in the village. 'And the cheese at Little Pond Farm is the best we'll ever taste.'

'I can vouch for both,' Glen said. 'And if you feel like a break from cooking while you're here, the food at The Frog and Lily is very good. Nothing fancy. Just the usual pub fare, only tastier than most. If you pop in on the carol evening, there's even a free buffet.'

'Thanks,' Christy said, 'but we can't really leave the children.'

'They're welcome in the pub. And you don't have to stay for long if you want to get them home to bed. Anyway, that's entirely up to you, of course. I'd better get on. I was actually on my way to Hettie's, when I saw you and the children playing and felt I wanted to come and say hello. Oh, you probably haven't met Hettie and her husband Fred yet, but she has one thing your children may like.' He leant forward conspiratorially. 'A pet white rat and he's called Prince Gustav.'

Christy shuddered dramatically. 'A pet rat? I'm not sure I like the sound of that.'

'He's perfectly harmless, and completely lovable,' Glen said, grinning. 'Much like Hettie and Fred. But a little word of warning about Hettie. She's lovely, as I said, but she believes in lots of myths and superstitions and she's also, let's just say, very interested in other people's business, so watch out for that. But she really is a dear old lady, and Fred is always keen to help. They live in

Duckdown Cottage just a little farther up the lane, two doors before Sunbeam Cottage, Mia's home.'

'That's good to know. Thanks.' Christy said, before glancing at Cathy. 'I thought you said Mia isn't at Sunbeam Cottage now?'

Cathy nodded. 'She's moved to Little Pond Farm, or so she said yesterday.'

'Ah yes.' Glen nodded his head and smiled. 'She's staying at Jet's for the holidays and renting out Sunbeam Cottage. She did mention it on Monday, but I had completely forgotten. Bye for now then. See you on Saturday I hope, if not before. Goodbye Daisy. Bye bye, Dylan.' He gave them a little wave.

'Daisy. Dylan. Say goodbye,' Cathy prompted, but they were far too busy falling backwards in the deep snow, making more snow angels and giggling their heads off, to take any notice.

Glen laughed. 'Don't worry. Let them have fun. There's nothing quite so heart-warming as seeing children playing and to hear that innocent laughter. You have lovely children.'

'Thank you,' Cathy and Christy said in unison, Cathy wishing that everyone felt that seeing Daisy playing and shrieking with laughter, was heart-warming.

Chapter Eighteen

After leaving Cathy, Christy and the children, Glen headed back up the lane but instead of going straight to Hettie's, he turned to his left and trudged through the deep, pristine snow on the village green, skirting around the ice-covered pond and leaving a tell-tale line of footprints directly to the door of Lake's Bakes. He hadn't really spoken to Jenny since Monday night when he walked her home, and thought that maybe today, when most people would be indoors because of the snow, would be a prime opportunity.

He had popped into the bakery on Tuesday to buy some cakes for those attending choir practice on Tuesday night, but the queue had been outside the door and Jenny clearly didn't have time to stop and chat. He had bought a selection of cakes, asked how she was, reminded her that she was more than welcome to come along and mime at choir practice, and then he had left. Jenny had been friendly and even smiled once or twice, but she definitely wasn't as keen to chat as she had been on Monday night, and she didn't come to join the choir.

On Wednesday, he hadn't been able to get out until the afternoon; his uncle, the Bishop, called with news in the morning which meant Glen had to fill out paperwork and write a report. It also meant he had to do some serious thinking and after that, he had decided that perhaps it was better to avoid Jenny Lake.

But as much as he had tried to stay away, he found he had a craving for cavallucci, and by mid-afternoon, it was a craving he could no longer resist. The sky looked ominous and the forecasted blizzard was well and truly on its way as he rushed from his cottage towards Lake's Bakes, only to find Hettie in there, chatting, and clearly in no hurry to leave.

'You can go before me, vicar,' Hettie generously offered.

'No, no,' Glen said, raising his hand to gesture that he wouldn't hear of such a thing. 'That's fine. I'm in no rush.'

Hettie raised her eyebrows. 'You looked in a rush to get here. We saw you racing across the green.'

'Racing? I wasn't racing. I was simply trying to get out of the cold. And as it's so warm in here, I'm in no hurry to leave.' He smiled and hoped they both believed him.

Jenny smiled back. 'It's not that warm in here, Glen. There's a definite draught coming from that door, even when it's closed. I'll be glad if this blizzard does arrive. It'll give me an excuse to close early and to go and sit in front of the fire in my cosy sitting room.'

Hettie looked shocked. 'Close early? But what if people want bread or cakes?'

Jenny smiled again but pulled a face. 'If this blizzard is as bad as they forecast, bread and cakes will be the last thing on people's minds, Hettie. And if they really are that desperate, they can always ring the doorbell. Most people know me well enough by now.'

Hettie clasped her hands beneath her bosom and pursed her lips. 'I suppose that's true. Good heavens.' She glanced through the bakery window. 'It's suddenly looking mighty dark out there. I think they're right about that blizzard. I'd better get home before it starts.'

No sooner had she said those words than it arrived, and in a matter of seconds the winds were whistling across the green and rattling the bakery door.

'I think you might get blown over out there, Hettie,' Jenny said. 'Perhaps Glen will be good enough to see you home. What can I tempt you with, Glen?'

'Oh. Yes of course,' he'd said, before mumbling his order of a loaf of bread and a bag of her mini gingerbread men.

Glen had cursed his luck. He hadn't be able to stop and talk to Jenny. He could hardly have let Hettie try to walk home alone, and by the time that he got back, Jenny had closed up. He had been more than tempted to ring the doorbell of Baker's Cottage, pretending that he had wanted something else in addition to the bread and biscuits, but he knew she would see it as an excuse to speak to her. Besides, the blizzard was really setting in and he decided it was best if he got home and in the warm. Where most sensible people already were.

During Wednesday evening, when it had sounded as if a tornado was tearing through Little Pondale, he had considered battling the elements and going to see if Jenny was okay, but it sounded like yet another pathetic excuse, even to him, and thankfully, his common sense prevailed.

This morning he had intended to go directly to Hettie and Fred's, but then he'd seen the children playing and he had a sudden urge to go and say hello. After that, he really had meant to go to Hettie's yet here he was, walking towards Lake's Bakes.

He smiled when he saw the window display. Hadn't Jenny said that Christmas was not her favourite time of year? For someone who didn't like Christmas, the window was looking very festive today. Iced, baked biscuits in the shape of stars, Christmas wreaths, holly leaves and Christmas trees hung in rows, dangling from red ribbons. They were interspersed with gingerbread men and women, 'dressed' with colourful icing and hanging from gold ribbons. Striped candy canes hung from green ribbons at each end and below all these gently swaying delights were trays of Christmas biscuits, mince pies, cavallucci, iced cinnamon swirls, mini pannetone, panforte, struffoli and many more delicious treats. He pushed open the bakery door and little silver bells jingled above his head.

'Hello, Glen,' Jenny said, beaming at him. You're my first customer today. What can I tempt you with?'

His mind went completely blank for a second or two. Why did she always have to use those words? Didn't she know the images they conjured up in his mind? Images that some might feel were inappropriate for a vicar.

'Um. Hello, Jenny. Gosh it's cold, but your bakery is looking very festive. I thought you didn't like Christmas?'

Jenny shrugged, before smiling warmly. 'It's the oddest thing. I've never liked Christmas. Not since becoming an adult, at least. But helping out at Jet's on Monday, and seeing all the decorations in the village made me feel as if I was a bit of a grouch. And it's been a very quiet morning so far, due to the weather, I assume. So I thought, why not? I only meant to make a few biscuits to hang up, but I seem to have got a bit carried away.' She laughed as she waved her arm in the air.

'Well it looks wonderful. And very welcoming, not to mention extremely tempting. But talking of the weather, did you get through the blizzard intact? I mean the cottage. Was there any damage? Several of the Christmas decorations in the lane have either blown down or fallen over. One of the reindeer on Mia's roof looks to be making a run for it. I must call and tell Jet about it. He'll want to make sure it's secure. We can't have reindeer flying about the village, can we?'

He was rambling again. He rather hoped he'd got past that after Monday night, but nope.

'Not until Christmas Eve,' Jenny replied, grinning. 'As for the blizzard. No damage, as far as I'm aware, thanks. It was a bit frightening though, wasn't it? At one point I was tempted to rush over to your place, just to have someone to talk to during the worst of it. But by the time I thought about it, I could hardly even see your cottage door. Then I realised that I couldn't simply turn up unannounced, merely because I was a little frightened by the weather.'

'You're welcome to turn up at my door anytime, Jenny, and you don't need an excuse. Not that I'm saying that was an excuse. What I meant was, you don't need a reason.'

Her eyebrows crinkled but she smiled. 'Thanks. That's kind of you. I'll bear that in mind. As it was, I turned my music up really loud on my iPad in my bedroom, and lounged in a warm bath of Christmas spice scented bubbles with Michael

144

Bublé and a glass of mulled wine. I can highly recommend it.' She winked at him and her smile grew wider.

Okay. Now she must be doing this on purpose. He'd have that image in his head all morning. Only he would be in the bath with her, and they wouldn't just be listening to music and drinking mulled wine.

He cleared his throat. 'That sounds like a perfect evening.'

'Almost.' She lowered her gaze. 'I've made some mince pies. They're sweet mincemeat, cranberries and orange, a bit like Hettie's only these have a dash of Grand Marnier added to the mixture. Would you like to try one?'

'I'll take three, please. I'm on my way to Hettie and Fred's right now. I didn't want to go empty-handed. Fred's kindly printing out carol sheets for Saturday evening. He really is a genius with Photoshop. He's making them into little booklets, with pictures of robins and holly and mistletoe and such. He said people could retain them, as keepsakes of the evening, which I think is a lovely touch. I'm pretty good with a computer but I can't do half the things he can. I'm going to hand them out today, and at the same time, check how people are coping in this snow. Some of the villagers are elderly and can't get out in it and they don't have anyone to run errands for them.'

'That's so kind of you, Glen. I know they'll appreciate it. Not many people would think of others the way you do.'

'Don't sound so impressed. It sort of goes with the territory.'

'Don't make light of it,' she scolded. 'You know as well as I do that not all vicars would go to such trouble.'

He shrugged. 'It's no trouble. This is a small village. It won't take me longer than an hour or two, and it beats writing reports or filling in forms.'

She looked him directly in the eyes. 'You're a kind man. There aren't many men like you these days.'

He gave an exaggerated frown. 'That makes me sound incredibly boring, somehow. Isn't that the sort of thing women say to a man who asks them out, when they're not interested but they don't want to be rude and simply say, 'Get lost, loser,' or something like that?'

'Well if it is, that wasn't how I meant it. I meant it as a compliment. No. It's not a compliment, it's a statement of fact. You are a kind man. You've been nothing but kind to me since the day we met. And believe me, Glen, that doesn't make you in the least bit boring. Quite the opposite, in fact.'

What did that mean? That it made him interesting? And if so, in what way? Was she telling him that she liked him? Or was she merely being friendly? There was only one way to find out.

'I thought I might pop into the pub tonight, if the weather doesn't get worse. If Michael Bublé's busy, you're welcome to join me.'

The silence was deafening and the look on Jenny's face told him all he needed to know.

'Join us, I meant,' he added hastily. 'It's rugby practice tonight. Somehow I managed to agree on Monday at the supper party that I'd go along and try out for the team. Jet said we all adjourn to the pub afterwards, but as the field is under two feet of snow, I suspect it'll be straight to the pub. Anyway, it's just a thought if you fancy getting out for the evening. And I'll happily walk you the two hundred yards or so home, or one of us will, I'm sure.'

Okay, he must shut up now. This hole he was digging himself was about to cave in.

'Thanks,' she said, visibly relaxing a little. 'But I'd planned to spend the evening in my kitchen. I've got some new recipes I want to try out for the festive season. Have fun though.'

She put the mince pies in a box and handed it to him. He gave her ten pounds in return and when she held out his change, he nodded towards the charity box on the counter, for a local animal sanctuary. 'Put it in there. See you tomorrow, I expect. Have a great day, Jenny.'

She smiled. 'Kind, you see.' She dropped the coins in the box. 'You have a great day too, Glen.

And don't let Hettie fill your head with stories. She told me one the other day about a Wishing Tree. It's up on Frog Hill, near Frog's Hollow. Did you know you mustn't go there on a Monday?'

He grinned at her and nodded. 'Yes. She's told me about the curse of Frog's Hollow. She also told me about the tree the other day. I'm afraid I don't believe in such things though so she was wasting her breath with me.'

'No. I don't suppose you would. And as if a tree could grant a wish anyway. What a lot of nonsense. See you soon.'

Oddly though, the look in her eyes as she said it made Glen wonder if that was what she really believed, but she didn't say anything more about it.

'Total nonsense,' he said. 'See you tomorrow.'

He gave her a final smile before shoving the door open and closing it quickly behind him to limit the draught. Then he made another path through the snow, this time around the other end of the pond and down and across the lane to Hettie and Fred's cottage, all the while envisioning Jenny and that bath and him, with Christmas music playing softly in the background.

Chapter Nineteen

Mia opened the door of Sunbeam Cottage and gasped. 'I told you not to come out in this weather, Hettie. Ella, Mum and I can manage. Jet, please take her home this minute. What are you still doing here anyway? I thought, after dropping us off and seeing the reindeer hanging from the roof, you were getting Gill to come and help secure it back in place?'

Jet raised his brows. 'That's exactly what I was doing. I was driving away when Hettie jumped out in front of me and virtually demanded I walk her to the door. And I know better than to argue with Hettie.' He shook his head and grinned as Hettie stepped into the hall.

'Jumped out in front of you indeed, deary. I did no such thing. You know that's how my dear Hector died. But it's the second time this week. Someone almost ran me down yesterday morning around this time. I think it's those people staying in Corner Cottage.' She clasped her hands beneath her bosom and pursed her lips, as usual, leaning forward as she did so. 'Single mothers, both of them, so I heard. The little ones are sweet though. Fred and I saw them playing in the snow early this morning, and the vicar had a chat with them. He says they are very nice. But then he would say that, wouldn't he? Anyway, I'm here now so let's get on. I want to help get this place spick and span before your second lot of guests arrive tomorrow. Assuming they can get here in this weather. But listen to me, talking ten chickens at a time. And what are you still doing here, young man? You're letting all the heat out and the cold air in.' She stared at Jet. 'Don't you have a farm to run? Just because your girlfriend's rich, it doesn't mean you can become a slacker now, you know.'

'A slacker?' Jet glared at her. 'I don't think you could ever accuse me of that, Hettie. And it's Mia's money, not mine, so the fact that Mia's rich doesn't affect my life in any way.'

'Oh goodness me. I've hit a nerve haven't I, deary?'

Jet sighed. 'No, Hettie. You haven't. But you're right. I do have a farm to run. Goodbye.' He leant forward, kissed Mia on the cheek and was gone before Mia could say goodbye in return.

'I have you know, deary.' Hettie nodded. 'Hit a nerve, I mean. You know how some men are. They don't like their partners having more money than them, and you know how stubborn that young man is.'

Mia had no idea what was going on. Jet hadn't seemed at all bothered about the money issue – until today. Or perhaps there was another problem. Perhaps he was already sick of her living at Little Pond Farm, even though she had only been there since yesterday. Perhaps after seeing the state his kitchen was in this morning had made him think. Or perhaps he was tired of ferrying her about, even though he had been the one to offer, saying he had four-wheel drive and his car could cope in this weather much better than hers. Or perhaps … Perhaps Hettie was simply wrong, and Jet was merely annoyed that once again, she was poking her nose into other people's business. He had worked so hard to get his farm. To call him a slacker would certainly rub him up the wrong way.

'Is that Hettie?' Ella asked, coming into the hall. 'You must be able to smell the teapot.'

'Oh? Am I in time for a cup of tea?' Hettie took off her hat and coat and handed them to Mia to hang up. 'I've just had one with the vicar, but I'm sure another one won't hurt. Well, come along now, deary. We haven't got all day.' She shooed Mia along the hall towards the kitchen. 'I'm convinced the vicar has his eye on our Jenny. Oh, hello Lori.' She pulled out a chair and sat beside Mia's mum. 'Did you see him at the supper party? He walked her to the door, you know. And he's in and out of that bakery like a cockerel in a chicken house. Not that dear Glen is anything like a cockerel. More like a mouse. At least he is when he's around Jenny. Goes all coy and tongue-tied, deary. But I've told them both about the Wishing Tree so if anything's to come of it, we'll soon find out.'

Ella put a cup of tea on the table in front of Hettie and refilled everyone else's cups. 'Er. Wishing Tree, Hettie? This is the first I've heard of a Wishing Tree. And what's it got to do with Jenny and Glen?'

Hettie looked surprised. 'Haven't I told you about the Wishing Tree? Deary me. Mind you, I suppose I thought you wouldn't be needing it, seeing as you're all so happily in love. It works for things besides Love, of course, but it grants more wishes for Love than anything else.'

'And?' Ella persisted as Hettie smiled and drank her tea.

'And what, deary? Oh. You mean you want to hear about it?'

Ella rolled her eyes and glanced at Mia.

'Yes, Hettie,' Mia said. 'We want to hear about it.' This was unusual for Hettie. She didn't usually require encouragement; she normally blurted everything out, whether you wanted to hear about it or not.

'Well, as I told both Jenny and the vicar, it's near Frog's Hollow, so no wishing on a Monday, remember. You can't miss it. It's an ancient oak and fairly rare for these parts because it's a white

152

oak. It often keeps its leaves in winter although they dry and turn a tan colour, making the tree look even more beautiful, deary. It sits alone on a small raised patch, just before you get to the pond. You make a wish and write it down and then place it at the foot of the tree, or tie it to a branch. No pins, only ribbon or string. Ribbon's so much nicer though. And you're asking the tree to grant your wish so the least you can do is tie it with something pretty, don't you agree, my dears? And if the tree decides to grant your wish, seven days later, it'll come true.'

'Seven days later?' Lori asked.

'Within seven days,' Hettie said. 'Some wishes take longer to grant than others.'

'So if your wish doesn't come true after seven days, it won't come true at all?' Ella asked.

Hettie nodded. 'Precisely, deary. And you mustn't ask twice. Not within the same year in any event. And it's only in December. The tree won't grant wishes any other month. You can ask on the last day of December and that's fine. But I think it's rude to ask for a wish at the very last minute, deary, don't you?'

Mia, Lori and Ella all exchanged glances.

'Absolutely,' Ella said, clearly stifling her laughter. 'I can understand the tree being rather annoyed by such bad manners.'

'I've got everything I could ever want,' Mia said, throwing Ella a reprimanding look. 'I don't think there's anything I need to wish for.'

Lori nodded. 'I feel the same.'

'Me too,' said Ella. 'I suppose.'

'Which is why I didn't need to tell you, my dears. Now Jenny and the vicar, on the other hand. They're an entirely different kettle of fish. There are one or two things those two could wish for, deary. I'm fairly sure about that.'

'Speaking of Jenny.' Mia got to her feet and grabbed her bag. 'I fancy something sweet with this tea. Shall I nip across the green and get some cakes?'

'That's a great idea,' said Ella. 'Better get a couple for Jet and Gill. They'll probably want a cake after they get down from the roof.'

Lori shook her head. 'They've got to get up onto the roof first. And with it covered in snow, I'm not sure that's an easy task.'

Mia frowned. 'But Jet said he'll be fine. He just needs to get the right ladders. God. The last thing we need is Jet or Gill to fall off a roof. Perhaps I should tell them to leave it.'

'Yeah. But on the other hand, you can't have a reindeer swinging by its neck when your guests arrive, can you?' Ella said. 'It's a bit macabre, don't you think?'

'You're right. And then there's the snowman on Corner Cottage. We can't risk that blowing off.'

Ella snorted with laughter. 'A farting snowman. Those kids will love that.'

Mia tutted. 'You know what I meant. We can't risk it blowing off the roof if we have another blizzard. Or even a strong wind. If it hits one of the kids, or the adults, or anyone in fact, we could be sued. Well, I could. But I don't want Jet to fall off the roof either.'

'There, you see deary,' Hettie said. 'There is something you could wish for. Not that you could wish for that today. Even the Wishing Tree needs a little bit of notice.'

Mia rolled her eyes. 'I'll go and get those cakes.' She went to the hall, put on her coat and gloves and headed towards Lake's Bakes.

'Morning, Mia!' a voice called out.

Mia turned to see Cathy walking up the lane towards her and she waited.

'Hello, Cathy. Jet and Gill will be popping down later to do something about the snowman. They won't disturb you, I hope, but if you hear footsteps on the roof, it's them, not Santa and his reindeer coming early.'

Cathy laughed. 'Thanks. I'll make sure I tell the kids or they'll be getting excited. And as we're on the subject of reindeer. Did that one decide he couldn't face another Christmas?' She pointed to the reindeer hanging off the roof of Sunbeam Cottage and smiled, before suddenly becoming serious as a far-away look appeared in her eyes. 'Sorry. That was in bad taste.'

'No, it wasn't. And you should've heard what Ella said about the snowman.' Mia rolled her eyes. 'Where are you off to?'

'I'm going to the bakery to get some crusty rolls, if they have them. We're having soup for lunch and there's nothing as nice as a warm crusty roll with a bowl of soup.'

'Jenny does the most delicious rolls. I'm headed there myself. I'll walk with you. Although I think we may need snowshoes to get across the green.'

Cathy nodded. 'The vicar made it earlier. You can see his footprints.' She pointed to the line of prints. The only line, save for several tiny prints made by various birds. 'He came and introduced himself, and invited us to the charity carol evening on Saturday, which was very nice of him. I told him you'd already invited us.'

'And you'll probably get more invitations as you meet more people. This is a very friendly village. For the most part.'

'It certainly seems to be. We're already glad we came. Your cottage is really lovely and I couldn't believe how peaceful it was this morning. Once the blizzard had stopped, of course.'

'That was one of the things we first noticed. We lived in London and on our first night here, we were a bit freaked out. It was as silent as the grave, but the foxes, owls and various other wildlife take a bit of getting used to, as well as the silence. Now, I can't imagine ever being able to sleep in London for all the noise. We're going up to spend one night in the New Year, so we'll see how we get on. Gill is taking us to see Swan Lake, the ballet. But that's another story and I don't know why I'm boring you with this.'

'It's not boring,' Cathy said. 'Don't tell Daisy about the ballet though. She's ballet mad. Or she was.' She cleared her throat. 'She had to give it up a couple of months ago.'

'That's a shame. Any particular reason?'

Cathy shrugged. 'Things have been a bit difficult. But we'll be fine now. And this holiday will do us all the world of good. I'm so pleased we found this cottage on the internet. I was getting pretty desperate.'

'I'm so sorry things haven't been going well. Hopefully they'll improve next year.'

'They will,' Cathy said, far more enthusiastically. 'At least I hope they will. No. They definitely will.'

Mia gave her a sideways glance. 'This is utter nonsense of course, but then again, the cave worked, so perhaps it might. Sorry. Thinking aloud. Um. There's a woman in the village called Hettie. She lives in Duckdown Cottage. That's the one there.' Mia turned around and pointed at it.

'Oh gosh. I nearly hit someone coming out of there, yesterday morning when we arrived. She appeared from nowhere. The vicar mentioned her this morning.'

Mia smiled. 'That was Hettie. And yes, Glen would. She's a bit of a character. And a gossip, but she's lovely when you get to know her.'

'He said she has a pet white rat.'

'Prince Gustav. Yes. He's gorgeous.'

'Sorry. You were saying?'

'Yes. Hettie is a bit of a one for superstitions. The curse of Frog's Hollow and such. She's just told us a new one. And I know it's all very silly, but sometimes there are things beyond our comprehension, and what we were saying about hoping next year will be better, reminded me. There's apparently a Wishing Tree where you can go and make a wish and within seven days, it'll come true. Or not. I'll tell you all about it and you can decide for yourself. But whatever you do, don't go there on a Monday. Don't worry. I'll explain all about that too.'

'A Wishing Tree? I like the sound of that. And I know exactly what I'd wish for.'

Chapter Twenty

The snow stopped shortly after Thursday lunchtime and the blanket of white was dappled with pale lemon rays of sunshine. Mia spent the afternoon helping Jet with things at the farm although all she really did was fill the chickens' feeders and water bowls and stand amongst some cows. In truth, she had been more of a hindrance than a help but Jet had been incredibly patient with her. Until she had mentioned the money.

'It doesn't bother you, does it? Me having all the money Mattie left me.' She was trying to catch a chicken at the time so it was possibly the wrong time to ask.

'Of course not. Why would it bother me? Concentrate on what you're doing or you'll end up flat on your face.'

'It shouldn't. But when Hettie mentioned it today, you snapped at her.' She caught a couple of tail feathers but they, and the bird, slipped through her fingers.

'I didn't snap at her. I merely set her straight because yet again, she was sticking her nose into someone else's business and getting the facts all wrong. You need to get your hands around the front and the wings, not grab at its tail.'

'She's always sticking her nose into people's business. That's what she does. But she doesn't always get it wrong. And you did snap. I really hope the money isn't an issue, Jet because you know how much I love you and the money is as good as yours as well as mine.'

'Can we please forget about Hettie and your money? Are you going to catch a chicken or just chase them around the barn? They're getting a little distressed and this isn't good for their blood pressure, or mine.'

She stopped and stood up straight. 'And now you're snapping at me. Is something wrong, Jet? Are you regretting suggesting I move in with you? It's only temporary. I'll leave on the 2nd of January.'

A startled look swept across his face. 'I'm not regretting anything. Except perhaps suggesting you try to pick up a chicken. Let's leave this for today. I'm cold and hungry and I'm tired. I need a long bath, a good meal and a very early night.'

'It's a good thing Gill's cooking dinner then,' she said, turning to walk away.

Jet grabbed her arm. 'Mia. I'm not regretting it. Honestly I'm not. I'm loving having you here. Well, not here in this barn if I'm going to be completely honest and the chickens aren't too keen either, so let's get out of here and let them settle down.' He grinned and pulled her into his arms, kissed her briefly on the lips and walked her towards the door. 'I'm loving having you here at the farm. It's just that Christmas is a difficult time for me. It's the anniversary of Mum's death and it always brings back memories.' He stopped to close the door behind them.

'Oh Jet. I'm so sorry. I didn't think of that.'

He shrugged and looked into her eyes. 'It's okay. They're happy memories mainly, but there are some sad ones too. And having the farmhouse full of people is making it feel different somehow. I don't expect you to understand this because I'm not sure I understand it myself. But it feels like a home again. And it hasn't felt like that since Mum was alive. I think it's made me miss her more, that's all.'

'I do understand, Jet. I still miss my dad and he's been gone for years. Christmas makes us miss those we love. But it should also make us value those we have, even more than we usually do. It's harder for you because this is also when she died, but surely having your house feel like a home again is a good thing, isn't it?'

He nodded. 'Yes. Of course it is. But it just feels odd, that's all.'

'So it's not about the money?'

He brushed a wisp of hair from her face and smiled into her eyes. 'It's not about the money. I couldn't care less about the money. And besides, if you didn't have the money, we wouldn't be getting four real live reindeer for Christmas would we? Assuming they can get here, of course.'

'They should be here by this time tomorrow.' Mia couldn't keep the excitement from her voice. 'And look. The snow's already melting and we've only had a couple of hours of sunshine. It feels warmer too, and the forecast for the morning is sunny spells, so let's keep our fingers crossed that they can make it here.'

Once again, the forecast was accurate and the sun rose with the dawn on Friday morning. The temperature shot up by several degrees and by lunchtime, the snow was noticeably starting to melt.

At exactly three p.m. on Friday afternoon, the reindeer arrived, along with Jane Doe, the lovely woman from the reindeer farm, who was going to teach Mia, Jet and everyone else at Little Pond Farm, how to look after them. Jet had said they should leave Little M indoors because they weren't sure how she would react to the arrival of the reindeer.

'Hello Jane,' Mia said, before Jane had even got out of the driver's seat of the horsebox. 'We're so excited to see the reindeer. And to meet you, of course.'

'Hi Mia. I'm happy to be here. Forty-five miles isn't a long way to come but the roads are still quite treacherous in places and it's taken some time to get here. I'd like to get the reindeer settled in before dark. May I see the barn? It looked perfect in the emails you sent, but I want to check before we begin to unload.'

'Of course. This is Jet. He owns the farm.'

Jane said hello to Jet and to everyone else as Mia introduced them.

'Is your name really Jane Doe?' Ella asked, grinning.

Jane grinned back. 'It is. So it was either a career with the police, or working with deer. I chose deer, because they're more fun.'

'The barn's this way,' Jet said, smiling at Jane, who followed him and Mia down the path.

'Love the reindeer,' Jane said, nodding at the twig reindeer beside the path. 'You certainly love Christmas, don't you?'

'Most of this is thanks to Mia,' Jet said, taking Mia's hand. 'I usually have a tree indoors and a few decorations, but this year we've pushed the boat out. Are you a fan of Christmas?'

'I love it. The more lights, the happier I am.'

They reached one of the smaller barns that had been used for storage, mainly silage, but due to the heat this summer silage stores were low and what was left had been moved to one of the other barns.

'This is perfect,' Jane said. 'They like to be outside during the day and any of the fields you pointed out will be fine. The snow won't bother them at all. In fact, they prefer cold weather so they'll be in their element. As I mentioned in my emails, their diet consists of grass, moss and lichen and I've brought that with me, as you requested. If you need more, I'll happily bring it over. Just so you know, a male reindeer is a buck, a female is a doe, of course, and a baby is a fawn. The sound they make is called a bellow. You'll know why when you hear it. Okay. This all looks ace. Let's introduce you to the deer and them to their new home for Christmas.'

They all trailed back to the horsebox and Jet helped Jane open the back door. Four pairs of large brown eyes stared out at them. Jane led them out, one by one.

'This silver-grey beauty is called Sparkle. She's got a personality to match. She's two years old.' She handed the lead to Jet while Mia said hello. 'This chocolate delight is Coco. She loves a cuddle and is a bit of a joker. She's also two.' Gill took her reins. 'And this is Doughnut. As you can see, she's a mix of silver grey and fawn. She can't make up her mind what colour she wants to be, and she can be a bit of a doughnut, so watch out for her doing silly things. She's three.' Franklin took the reins of Doughnut. 'And finally, this is Diamond Dancer. White reindeer such as this are very rare. Only one in several thousand deer is born white. They're considered to be lucky. When she walks, it looks as if she's dancing. She's the most graceful out of all of them, and can be a bit of a diva. She's special and she knows it. All of them are happy to pull a sleigh, although Diamond Dancer may need a little bit of a treat to persuade her. An apple or a carrot will do the trick. Right let's get them to the barn.'

Jane led the way, showing them how to hold the reins and how to remove them once the deer were safely in the barn. Lori and Ella nipped back to the farmhouse to make mugs of hot chocolate and brought them out to the barn where everyone drank it and ate some mince pies Mia had bought from Jenny's earlier that morning, while they all watched the reindeer sniff the air, and investigate their new home. Then Jane gave Mia, Ella and Lori some moss to feed the reindeer.

'They're very gentle creatures,' Jane said. 'Just feed them as you would your cows, Jet, only with the food I've brought. They eat fresh grass too, but they won't get much of that this Christmas. Here's an information sheet I printed out.' She handed it to Mia. 'It tells you all you need to know. You said there's a vet in the village?'

Mia nodded. 'Yes. He's very good, although I don't think he's dealt with reindeer before, but when we told him we were hoping to have some over Christmas, he said he'd do some swotting up. Just in case.'

'That's excellent. I'm sure they'll be fine, but feel free to call me anytime, day or night, if you're worried about anything. Their health and happiness is my prime concern, so please don't hesitate to call. Even if you think it's something silly. Better to be wrong than sorry.'

'We'll take really good care of them, I promise,' Mia said. 'And you're sure it's okay for them to pull the sleigh in the village, like I told you?'

'Absolutely. We hire reindeer out all the time to do exactly that. And from what you've told me, there isn't much traffic in your village.'

'Hardly any,' Mia confirmed. 'Especially now, with this snow. You'll be lucky to see one car a day.'

'Right then.' Jane went and hugged, kissed and patted each deer in turn. 'I'll say goodbye and get back to our farm. Don't forget to call if you need me. Or just call to let me know how things are going. I'd love to see photos if you do get that sleigh and do what you said you'd like to do. We have a massive board at the farm where we stick photos like that.'

'I will,' Mia said, as she and Jet walked Jane back to the horsebox, leaving everyone else still mesmerised by the new residents at Little Pond Farm.

They waved Jane goodbye and when the vehicle was finally out of sight, Jet spun Mia to face him and wrapped his arms around her.

'So if the sleigh does arrive tomorrow, who, exactly are you going to get to play Father Christmas? And please don't look at me, because that's one role that I'm really not cut out for, especially as I've got black hair.'

Mia laughed. 'You could wear a wig. You'd have to wear a body suit to make you look fat. But don't worry. I'm not thinking of you. I'm actually thinking of Fred. And Hettie can be Mrs Claus. They're perfect for the parts.'

Jet nodded. 'You're right. They are. And Hettie can hand out presents, instead of her usual unwanted advice.'

'Now don't be mean, Jet. It's Christmas.'

'It is. And I fancy another very, very early night,' he said, his eyes twinkling and a devilishly sexy smile on his lips. 'Last night did me the world of good.'

'But we didn't get much sleep.' Mia looked into his eyes and smiled. 'And it's only five o'clock.' She kissed him on the lips but quickly pulled away. 'Oh my God. It's five o'clock! The Hardmans will be arriving in precisely thirty minutes. I've got to get to Sunbeam Cottage and light the fire and turn on the lights and make sure everything's ready. And I haven't packed their welcome box yet.'

'Don't panic. I can help. And look. Ella's running up the path and pointing to her watch. She's actually remembered something for once.'

She had remembered, and with Ella and Jet's help, Sunbeam Cottage was warm and welcoming by the time the Hardmans arrived, which wasn't until six.

'I apologise for being late,' a tall, blond, agile-looking man said, getting out of his Land Cruiser and smiling at Mia. 'The traffic was horrendous. It's the Friday before Christmas and everyone is heading off on their holidays, it seems. Hi. I'm Leo. Leo Hardman. You must be Mia.'

'Hello Leo,' Mia said, taking the hand he offered and receiving a firm handshake. 'This snow doesn't help. It's melting fast, but the roads around here are taking a long time to clear.' He was around Jet's age; thirty-six, or possibly a few years older and he had a lovely, friendly smile and intense, deep green eyes.

'This is Hal, my brother, and our parents, Elizabeth and Alistair.'

Hal looked nothing like Leo, who obviously took after his mother, but Hal was the spitting image of Alistair, with dark auburn hair, and the palest, hazel eyes. Elizabeth's eyes were the same as Leo's except colder somehow, and her smile was nowhere near as friendly. Neither was her manner.

'The cottage is beautiful,' Elizabeth said, her lip curling slightly. She had an air of disdain about her and looked positively horrified when her gaze alighted on the Christmas decorations, especially the ones on the roof.

168

'I hope the decorations aren't too OTT,' Mia said. 'As I explained to your son on the phone, someone else was expected to be spending Christmas here, and we decorated accordingly, but due to a change of plans, we gave you this cottage as it's a little nicer than Corner Cottage and had suddenly become available.'

Ella gave Mia a questioning look, but thankfully, didn't say a word.

'I see,' Elizabeth said. 'And you didn't think to remove them?'

'The decorations are lovely,' Leo said. 'Very festive. And that's what this Christmas is all about.'

'Well let's get you inside in the warm,' Mia said, leading the way. 'There's a little welcome pack in the kitchen, and some instructions and information on where everything is and how it all works.'

'That's great,' Hal said, a hint of sarcasm in his tone. 'I'm sure we'll figure it all out. I saw the pub as we drove up. Is that really the only place in the village to get a drink? No wine bars or cocktail bars, or decent restaurants?'

Mia shook her head. 'That's the only place. The nearest town is about fifteen miles away. I did make that clear on the website. I hope that won't be a problem.' She kept her smile fixed in place.

'It serves good food,' Jet added, as Mia opened the front door and stood aside to let them in. 'And the bakery can match any you'll find in London.'

'And Jet's cheese is famous for miles around,' Ella added, following them all into the hall. 'You can get milk, fresh eggs, butter and cheese from Little Pond Farm. I've drawn you a map of everything in the village.'

'That couldn't have taken long.' Hal was smiling, but Mia wanted to give him a slap.

'Ignore my brother,' Leo said. 'He's a city boy through and through. The countryside and particularly a village like this are his absolute nemesis, but I thought it might do us all some good. We never seem to spend any time together these days.'

'Yes,' Elizabeth said, putting her arm around Hal. 'My darling boy is only here because Alistair and I are celebrating our Ruby Wedding anniversary, and we actually met in this village, many years ago. Leo has a rather romantic disposition and thought he would surprise us with this … treat. And what a surprise it was when I realised our destination. I thought it might have changed, but I can see it's exactly as it was all those years ago. It's like stepping back in time.' She didn't look at all happy about it. 'Darling Hal goes along with everything, dear Leo does, so he's here for Leo, and for us, of course, not because he wants to spend Christmas in a tiny village.' She smiled at Mia but Mia wasn't sure if Elizabeth was agreeing with her son or making excuses for his rudeness. She was being equally as rude.

'That's how I felt until I lived here,' Mia said. 'I never thought I'd want to live anywhere but London. Until I came here. Now I wouldn't want to live anywhere else.'

Hal gave a snort of derision. 'I don't expect you'd say that if you had a few million quid in the bank.' He sauntered into the living room and glanced around.

Mia clenched her fingers but she beamed at him when he turned back to face her.

'Actually, Hal. I do have a few million quid, as you put it. Several million, in fact. And I still wouldn't dream of moving away from this village. I love everything about it and everyone in it. I hope you'll enjoy your stay. My phone number's with the welcome pack, should you need to call. We'll say good evening, unless there's anything else you'd like to ask.'

Hal's face was a picture but Leo looked a little cross and when Mia turned to leave, he followed her outside.

'Please excuse my brother,' he said. 'Sometimes he forgets his manners. And I thought Mum would love to come back here, but I think I may have misjudged her enthusiasm for the place.' Leo was definitely being sincere. Mia could see that from his eyes. They were such expressive eyes.

She smiled at him and relaxed. 'And sometimes I forget mine. It's fine. I hope you do enjoy your stay, but if you've made a mistake and feel you want to leave, please tell me and we'll sort something out. It's Christmas and I'd hate for any of you to be unhappy here.'

'There's a pub. The cottage is gorgeous and it backs onto a beach. We've brought food and wine and if there's anything Hal, or Mum, can't live without, London's not that far away. I'm sure we'll have a great time, Mia. Have a wonderful Friday night. And thank you for the welcome pack.'

'My pleasure, Leo. You have a wonderful Friday night too.'

'You didn't mention the carol evening tomorrow,' Ella said, as they walked back to Jet's car.

'I noticed that,' Jet said. 'That Hal's an arrogant little shit, isn't he? And as for the mum. Well. I'm glad I didn't have a mum like that. She looked as if she'd just stepped out of one of those upmarket magazines and had misplaced her pedestal. And it was abundantly clear that Hal is her favourite son, wasn't it? I actually felt a bit sorry for Leo. He seemed like a nice guy.'

'Yes,' Mia said. 'The father didn't say a word. Did you spot that? Elizabeth clearly rules that roost. And I didn't mention the carol evening because I want it to be fun. I can't see the Hardmans trudging through snow, swinging lanterns and singing along with the locals, can you? Apart from maybe Leo.'

Chapter Twenty-One

The sky was blue and there wasn't a cloud to be seen when Mia got up on Saturday morning. She had received a call last night from the store where she'd ordered the sleigh, advising her the sleigh would be delivered by lunchtime on Saturday, weather permitting, so despite her longing for more snow, she was pleased to see the sunshine.

She had discussed her idea with Fred and Hettie, who were more than happy to play Father Christmas and Mrs Claus. Ella and Gill were taking them to the fancy dress shop in Little Whitingdale this morning, to find appropriate outfits. And Hettie had suggested that Prince Gustav play a part.

'He could be an elf,' Hettie had said.

'An elf?' Ella rolled her eyes. 'Of course, he could. Why not?'

'I like the idea,' Mia said.

'Of course you do,' said Ella.

174

'Will you need someone to drive the sleigh?' Mia asked. 'Or whatever you do with sleighs.'

'I can handle the reindeer,' Fred said. 'I used to do some carriage racing in my younger days. Reindeer are a bit like a cross between a horse and a cow. It shouldn't be a problem.'

'You're simply full of surprises, Fred,' Ella said.

Hettie had chuckled. 'You should see him in the bedroom.'

That had brought that conversation to an abrupt halt as both Mia and Ella exchanged glances and simultaneously said they had to be somewhere else.

'God,' Ella said, as they virtually ran down the drive of Duckdown Cottage, 'Can you imagine Hettie and Fred in the bedroom?'

'I can, but I'd really rather not. Let's get some cakes from Jenny's and go home.'

'Good idea. Not that I can face food after what I've just heard.'

They hurried to Lake's Bakes where Mia was surprised to see Cathy and Christy and their kids standing at the end of a queue. She was even more surprised to see that Leo Hardman who was in the queue in front of them, turned around, smiled at the little group and stepped aside to let them go before him.

'Am I imagining things,' Ella asked, 'or did Leo Hardman just let Cathy and Christy go ahead of him?'

'You're not imagining it.'

'It's weird how one brother can seem so nice and the other is a complete and utter plonker.'

'I couldn't have said it better myself. And yet yesterday, the mum was all over the horrid one, but didn't take much notice of Leo, as Jet pointed out. Isn't it typical that the awful one is her favourite and the nice one gets ignored?'

Ella nodded. 'Yeah. At first I thought the mum was nice but whenever she opened her mouth, I couldn't be sure if she was being friendly but foolish, or merely sarcastic.'

'Same here. I wonder how and where the mum and dad met? I know it was in this village, but why were they here and where were they staying?'

'I'm not sure I care,' Ella said. 'And I think I'll be happy when they leave. I wonder who's sleeping in my bed? It'd better not be the evil brother.'

'If it is, we'll give your bed to charity and buy you a new one. Hello Cathy, Christy, and Leo. And these two gorgeous girls must be Daisy and Dylan. Hello.'

Everyone exchanged greetings and Dylan held out a crocheted bunny.

'Who's this?' Leo asked, bending down to eye level with Dylan.

Mia and Ella looked at one another in surprise and so did Cathy and Christy, Mia noticed.

'Wabbit,' Dylan replied, sticking her forefinger in her mouth and twisting her little body to and fro.

Leo smiled. 'Hello wabbit. I'm Leo.'

'Le-o,' Dylan said, darting a look up at her mum.

'And who's this?' Leo asked Daisy, who was clutching a bear.

Daisy seemed a little shy and backed away a couple of inches. Leo appeared to notice because he moved back too, increasing the gap between them.

'I had a bear very similar when I was around your age,' he said. 'In fact, I've still got him. His name is Ulysses. He was a very adventurous bear but he's old now and doesn't get out much. His favourite drink is hot chocolate and he loves a sticky bun. One of those ones with lots of icing on. What does your bear like?'

Daisy gave a tiny smile. 'Barney likes hot chocolate too. But he hasn't had a sticky bun.'

'No?' Leo's green eyes were alight with amusement and Mia was mesmerised by him. So were the others it seemed because no one was saying a word. 'Well, Daisy and Barney, we'll have to do something about that, won't we? Sticky buns all round, I think, don't you?'

Daisy glanced at Cathy who smiled at her and Daisy quickly nodded. 'Yes,' she said. 'Yes please. Do you live here?'

'No. I'm here for Christmas. Do you?'

Daisy shook her head. 'No.' She pointed down the lane towards Corner Cottage. 'We're here for Christmas too. There's a snowman on the roof and candy canes in the garden. And me and Dylan built a snowman but it's melted nearly.'

'Oh, that's a shame. I'll tell you what. If we get more snow, I'll come and help you build another one. There's one on the roof where we're staying. And also reindeer.'

'Reindeer?' Daisy's eyes lit up. 'Dylan. There's a reindeer on his roof.'

'Four of them,' Leo corrected, grinning.

'Four?' Daisy sounded so excited and Dylan's eyes were huge.

'Guess what?' Mia said, unable to resist any longer. 'We've got real live reindeer at Little Pond Farm.'

Daisy and Dylan looked at one another and shrieked with delight. 'Real ones?' Daisy asked.

Mia nodded. 'And tonight they'll be in the village with a very special guest.'

The children shrieked again and Leo got to his feet, his brows raised as he smiled at Mia.

'I'm impressed. Real reindeer? You didn't mention those last night.'

'They're not ours. We've only got them for Christmas.'

'Will they be with the carol singers?' Cathy asked.

'Carol singers?' Leo interrupted. 'There'll be carol singers in the village tonight?'

'Yes,' Mia said. 'And yes, Cathy. The reindeer and the special guest will be with the carol singers. I believe we're starting at five-thirty from The Frog and Lily and we'll be coming down the lane to Corner Cottage first, then turning around and going across this green to here and then around towards the church and up to the cottages on Frog Hill. I think your girls may particularly like the special guest and his wife.' She winked at her.

Cathy's brows furrowed momentarily and then she beamed at Mia. 'Oh. I see. That's wonderful. We'll definitely be coming tonight then.'

'Excuse me,' Leo said. 'Is everyone invited to this evening, or is it by invitation only?'

'Everyone's invited,' Mia said. 'Provided they want to have fun.'

'Yes,' Ella said. 'Tell your brother.'

Leo grinned. 'Tell him what? To come, or not to come?'

'Ah,' Ella said. 'That is the question. Or something like that anyway.'

'Hal's great,' Leo said. 'Once you get to know him. I'm not sure carols are really his thing though, but I'll ask him. But if I may, I'd very much like to come.'

'You may,' Mia said, smiling, as the queue moved forward.

'Excellent,' replied Leo. 'I'm already looking forward to it.'

'So am I' said Christy, who had been oddly quiet until then. 'And did you say you have a brother?'

'I do.' Leo gave her a curious look. 'Do your husbands like carols? Or am I jumping to conclusions by asking about husbands?'

'I never married,' Christy said. 'And Cathy is a widow.'

That surprised Mia clearly as much as it did Ella and Leo.

'My daddy's in heaven,' Daisy said. 'But he watches over me, doesn't he, Mummy? And now my great-grandad's gone there too.'

Cathy nodded and Mia spotted a tear forming in her eye. 'He does, darling. And he always will. So will Grandad.'

'I'm so sorry,' Leo said hastily. 'That was a really stupid question. I truly apologise.'

'No need.' Cathy shook her head but seemed to be avoiding eye contact.

'I'm sorry too,' Mia said. 'I had no idea.'

Cathy shrugged. 'That's because I hadn't told you. My husband's been gone for three years now. My grandad died two months ago. I'm still a little raw.' She blinked back her tear and Leo presented her with his handkerchief.

'Me and my big mouth,' he said. 'I think I owe you more than a sticky bun or two right now.'

Cathy took the hanky. 'You don't owe me anything. Thank you for this.' She quickly wiped her eyes and then bent down and hugged Daisy.

'Mummy always gets upset when she talks about Daddy, or Grandad, doesn't she darling?'

Daisy nodded. 'And when Uncle Keith gets cross.'

'Daisy!' Christy snapped, but she smiled hastily and bent down and joined in the hug, pulling Dylan into it. 'We all get upset sometimes. Oh look. We're nearly first in the queue. Let's get some really yummy cakes for tea tonight, shall we?'

Daisy nodded. 'And sticky buns,' she said, glancing up at Leo who now had a strange look on his face.

'Definitely the sticking buns,' he said, smiling down at her before turning his gaze on Cathy, who had paled visibly. 'And I'm paying for whatever else you're having.' Cathy shook her head but he continued: 'I insist. It's my treat for being a jerk.'

'You're not a jerk,' she said, standing upright and handing him back his expensive-looking handkerchief, while holding Daisy's hand in hers.

'Keep it.' His smile grew even bigger. 'It's Christmas. And I hope it'll be a very happy one for all of us.'

'I rather think it might be,' Christy said, glancing from Cathy to Leo and finally to Mia. 'I feel it in my bones.'

'I'm sure it will be,' Mia said.

She had no idea who the uncle Keith was that Daisy mentioned, but clearly that black eye that

Lori had spotted on Cathy, wasn't given to Cathy by her husband.

But more important than that, Mia had seen the way Leo had looked at Cathy and the way she had looked at him. From what Christy had said, and the way she had behaved, Christy had seen it too. This was turning into an extremely interesting, and possibly rather eventful, Christmas.

Chapter Twenty-Two

It started snowing heavily again around two, and by four on Saturday afternoon, all the snow that had melted had been replaced with possibly a few more inches.

'If it carries on like this,' Cathy said, moving away from the kitchen window and over to the kettle. 'We won't be able to find you, Dylan. The snow will be over your head.' She laughed and ruffled Dylan's curls and Dylan giggled in response. 'Or you, Daisy.'

'I'm bigger,' Daisy said, extending her neck and back as far as she possibly could while seated at the kitchen table.

'You're taller, darling,' Cathy corrected. 'And you're both covered in glitter.' She laughed even louder. 'You're supposed to be getting that on the crackers, not on yourselves.'

'We are, Mummy. But it's sticky, look.' Daisy picked up the bottle of glue, squeezed some onto her hands, threw a handful of glitter over it and then slapped her glitter and glue-covered hand onto the body of the cracker, rolling it around.

Christy joined them from the hall and laughed. 'You're meant to put the glue on the cracker, Daisy and then sprinkle some glitter over it. Not on your hand.'

Dylan chortled with delight. 'Silly Daisy.' But she was similarly covered in glitter and glue and, spreading her little fingers wide and holding her hands up in the air, added, 'Silly Dylan.'

'And silly me for not keeping a closer eye on you,' Cathy said. 'We'd better get you two in the bath. You can't go out covered in glue and glitter.'

'I've made one for that nice man,' Daisy said, pointing to a cracker brimming over with pink, purple and gold glitter. 'The one who gave us sticky buns.'

'That's lovely of you, darling. I'm sure he'll be delighted.' Cathy threw Christy a huge grin.

'He was a nice man, wasn't he, Daisy?' Christy said. 'I think Mummy liked him.'

Cathy gasped but Daisy nodded.

'I liked him too. So did Barney.'

'So did I,' Christy said, walking towards the kettle and standing next to Cathy. Lowering her voice she added, 'But Cathy liked him a lot, didn't you Cathy?'

Cathy shot her a sideways glance. 'What gave you that impression? I hardly even noticed him.'

'Are you denying it?'

184

'Did you see his clothes? And the ring he was wearing on his little finger? It may have been small and not at all ostentatious but I know expensive jewellery when I see it. His watch alone probably cost more than my car. That thing was solid gold. And his shoes...' She shook her head and whistled. 'You don't get shoes like that on the High Street.'

Christy smirked. 'Yes. As you said. You hardly noticed him at all. I wonder if his brother looks like him.'

Cathy tutted. 'Okay, so I liked him. But the last thing I need is another man in my life right now. Besides, he wouldn't be interested in a woman like me. Especially not a woman with my baggage.' She made tea for herself and Christy, who got the milk from the fridge and two cartons of juice for Dylan and Daisy.

Christy pushed the straws into the juice cartons and handed them to the children, who instantly got them covered in glitter and stuck to their hands. Cathy tossed her a wet cloth and she did her best to remove some of the icky mess, but gave up, shaking her head.

'It'll come off in the bath.' Christy washed her hands and then returned to Cathy's side and poured the milk into their tea. 'Who said anything about having him in your life? Dogs may not be just for Christmas, but men definitely can be.' She nudged Cathy's arm. 'I saw the way you looked at one another. It's about time you had some fun. And some s-e-x.'

Cathy gasped again. Louder this time. 'I can't have s-e-x with him. I've got Daisy to think about.'

'You can think about Daisy and still have s-e-x. Only don't think about her while you're having it. That's just weird.'

'S-e-x,' Daisy repeated, sprinkling more glitter over another cracker and leaning her head from side to side. 'S-e-x.'

'Great,' said Cathy, frowning at Christy. 'She'll be repeating that all night now. Daisy, darling. Do you know what that means?'

'Yes Mummy.' She didn't break her concentration or even so much as turn her head around. 'It means a man and a woman like each other.'

'That's not exactly what it means, darling. But it's not a word we should say in public until we're older. Okay?'

'Older like you, Mummy?'

'Yes, darling.'

'Okay, Mummy.'

Christy grinned. 'There. Problem over. But I still think you should have some and I'll happily look after Daisy for the night, should you change your mind.'

'Thanks. But I won't be changing my mind. As much as I'd like to have some s-e-x, I don't think there's much chance of that, this Christmas.

Although the same goes for you. I'll look after Dylan for the night.'

'I might take you up on that. Depending on what the brother looks like. And we'd better get these girls into the bath when they've finished their juice. The carol singing starts in an hour.'

Chapter Twenty-Three

'I'm looking forward to this,' Hettie said, smoothing down her red velvet gown and matching coat and adjusting Fred's fake white beard and moustache to make them look as real as possible while he fixed his long white wig and Santa hat firmly in place.

Mia and Ella arranged a thick, white fake fur rug around Hettie's knees, and Fred's, and Lori and Franklin secured the massive sack of presents on the back of the red and gold painted sleigh. Mia had bought all the presents. She felt it was the least she could do for the villagers this Christmas. The presents for children were wrapped in colourful paper with glittery snowmen on for the boys and sparkly reindeer for the girls. Teenagers would get the presents wrapped in shiny blue paper for boys and glittery red for girls. The ones for the adults were wrapped in a variety of paper, but the gift tags from Santa were silver for the men and gold for the women.

Jet and Gill made sure the reindeer harnesses fitted perfectly and wouldn't rub or irritate the friendly beasts, who looked resplendent in their coats of red and gold and the rows of jingling gold-effect bells hanging from their reins. It had finally stopped snowing but the entire village was blanketed in white once more from the heavy snow that afternoon.

'Are we ready?' Glen said, standing behind the sleigh but in front of several carollers, all dressed in the costumes they wore every year. Most of them resembled characters from a Charles Dickens' novel – the wealthy characters, of course. Ella said that she and Gill were Scrooge's nephew and his wife, but Mia said that she and Jet were more like Poldark and Demelza, because of Jet's black hair and because she liked the name Demelza.

'That's not a Dickens' novel,' Ella said. 'That's Winston Graham.'

'I know. I'm just saying that's who we look like.'

Lori smiled. 'Franklin and I look like Lori Ward and Franklin Grant, dressed up in old clothes.'

'Yes. We're ready Glen,' Mia said as Toby, who looked rather dapper in his costume, handed out the lanterns containing battery-operated candles and Mia, Ella and Lori, formed a row behind the sleigh but ahead of Glen. Jet, Gill and Franklin formed another row behind their respective partners, with Little M by Jet's side, wearing her Santa hat from Monday night and an additional Santa 'jacket' that Mia had found in town when she and Ella were buying all the presents to go in the sleigh. The men were carrying lanterns in one hand and charity boxes for notes, in the other. The women held lanterns in one hand and with the other, were to take presents from the massive sack and hand them to Hettie to give out along the way.

Fred switched on the battery-operated lights around the sleigh and with a flick of the reins, the reindeer all trotted from the car park at the rear of The Frog and Lily out onto Lily Pond Lane. The carollers walked behind the vicar and the sleigh and burst into 'Silent Night', which was a contradiction in terms because tonight was going to be anything but silent.

Crowds of villagers lined the lane, far more than Mia could actually recall living in the village, but the more the merrier as far as she was concerned. She had made sure there were more than enough presents to go around. They were only small gifts, like Christmas-themed socks or ties, bath products, small toys or games and such, but it added a nice touch, especially for the children.

The procession made its way slowly down the lane, stopping for a minute or so at each cottage. That was just long enough for people to come and put some money into a second, much smaller, plainer sleigh, which was being pulled by a pair of Huskies owned by a friend of Bear's. He had turned up at the very last minute offering his services and Mia and the vicar simply couldn't resist. The Huskies and the second sleigh were at the back of the procession. Everyone was given a present by Hettie, whether they made a donation or not.

'Christmas is all about giving,' Mia said.

'Remember that when we go to bed tonight,' Jet replied, leaning over Mia's shoulder, with a wink and a grin.

Mia tutted. 'You used to say that I was the one who was always going on about sex. Now it's you.'

He shrugged. 'What can I say? Guilty as charged. And it's your fault for making me fall in love with you. Are you complaining?'

Mia grinned. 'No. I'm merely stating a fact.'

When the procession stopped outside Sunbeam Cottage, the Hardmans all stood at the end of the drive, but only Leo was smiling.

'Hello all,' he said, stepping forward and slipping several notes into the box Jet was holding rather than merely throwing a handful of coins into the sleigh. 'This is simply wonderful.'

'Yes,' Elizabeth said, from a little way behind him, and tossing a coin into the sleigh. 'It's simply …' Her voice trailed off as her brows drew together and she looked at Hettie, who in turn was staring at Leo, although gawking would be a better word for the expression on Hettie's face.

'Go and get your present, Leo,' Mia said.

He laughed and shook his head. 'I don't need a present, thank you. Give mine to one of the children.'

'You give it to one of them,' Mia said. 'You have to take one.'

'Okay, okay.'

He laughed and walked up to Hettie. Her mouth was now wide open and her eyes were virtually bulging in their sockets.

Leo stood before her but she didn't hand him a present; she merely stared at him.

Eventually she spoke. 'Hector?' she said, her voice just above a croak. 'Hector, is that you?'

Mia glanced at Jet. 'There's something wrong with Hettie. She thinks Leo's Hector.'

'I know,' Jet replied, furrowing his brows. 'But the odd thing is, Leo does look a lot like Hector. Well, what Hector looked like years ago. I've seen photos of him about the same age and believe me, Leo could be his twin. She'll realise in a moment.'

But she didn't. She continued staring and Leo looked a little uncomfortable.

'Hello,' he said, holding out his hand. 'My name's Leo. Leo Hardman. I think you have me confused with someone else.'

Hettie shook her head and Mia stepped forward while Fred slipped an arm around his wife and kissed her on her cheek.

'You okay, Love?' Fred asked.

'Hettie?' Mia said. 'Hettie. Are you okay?'

'Hettie?' Elizabeth Hardman gasped, edging closer to the sleigh. And then, she mirrored Hettie's look of disbelief. 'Hettie! Oh, dear God! I assumed you would be dead by now.'

'Elizabeth!' Hettie forced her gaze, clearly with some effort, from Leo to the woman standing by his side. 'Well, well. What dragged you back here?' And then once again she stared at Leo. 'Does this mean—?'

'Yes,' Elizabeth snapped, wrapping an arm around Leo's shoulder and pulling him away. 'This is my son. His name is Leo Hardman. I'd like you to remember that. And that it's the season of goodwill. Perhaps we can … catch up later.'

'Yes,' Hettie said. 'We should do that.' Her voice was cold, yet emotional.

'What's going on?' Leo asked, at the same time as Hettie's husband, Fred.

'Nothing,' Both Hettie and Elizabeth said in unison.

'Come along, Fred.' Hettie tapped Fred's arm. 'We've got presents to distribute.' She glowered at Elizabeth as Fred coaxed the reindeer forward but her eyes were warmer when they settled on Leo and she turned her head to look at him until Elizabeth pulled him out of sight.

'What was that about?' Mia asked, having watched Hettie the entire time. She now left plenty of space between them and the sleigh so that Hettie wouldn't hear.

Ella shrugged. 'Search me.'

'Unless I'm very much mistaken,' Lori said. 'I think Hettie and Elizabeth have a mutual past. Or should I say, a mutual person in their pasts. Hettie's first husband, Hector.'

'Do you mean what I think you mean?' Jet asked, leaning forward to see Lori clearer.

'I mean that Hettie knows Elizabeth from the past and Hettie thought Leo was Hector, her dead husband. Unless Hector had a brother we don't know about, I'd say there's a very strong chance that Leo's dad may not be the person Leo thinks he is.'

'Oh. My. God,' said Mia staring from her mum to Jet and back again. 'You mean Hector had an affair with Elizabeth and Leo is Hector's son. But Elizabeth's about your age, Mum?'

'And older men have been having affairs with much younger women since the beginning of time. Besides, look at me and Franklin. He's thirty-seven and I'm sixty. It works both ways, my darling. I may be wrong, of course. We'll have to wait and see.'

'Bloody Nora!' Ella said. And she hadn't said that for a long time.

194

Chapter Twenty-Four

'What was that about, Mum?' Leo asked, watching the sleigh move forward and seeing the strange, elderly woman still staring at him and the curious looks that Mia and her friends were also giving him.

'Nothing for you to worry about, my darling boy. But although you meant this with the best intentions, I think perhaps it was a mistake to come here.'

'She called me Hector, Mum, and she stared at me as if she knew me.'

'She's old. People lose their minds when they're old. You probably reminded her of someone and in her confused state of mind, she called you by that person's name. Let's not make a drama over something so simple as a case of mistaken identity.'

'You knew her, Mum. You said her name and she said yours. And you asked her to remember that I'm your son. What did that mean? I know there's more to this than you're saying.'

Elizabeth let out a sigh of irritation. 'Yes, okay. I knew her once, many years ago. She was a nasty gossip and she made life difficult for me. We never liked one another. That's all there was to it. Now let's go inside. It's bitterly cold out here and this parade is frankly, a joke. Where are Hal and your father? Oh. There they are. Talking to some of the locals. Come along, Leo.'

He shook his head. 'No, Mum. I want to go for a walk. And then I'm going to the pub. There's a buffet later and everyone will get together. You should come. It'll give you and that woman, Hettie, I think you called her, a chance to catch up. Bury the hatchet, perhaps? It is Christmas after all. The season of goodwill and all that. And it'll give me a chance to ask her why she was staring at me as if she'd seen a ghost.'

'No Leo! Don't go near that woman. Please, darling. For me? She won't have a good word to say about me, I can promise you that and she'll fill your head with lies, just the way she always did. There's a woman like that in every village. That's what makes them such dreadful places to live. Promise me you won't go near her. Please my darling. Promise me.'

He sighed and looked her in the eyes. She seemed close to tears and he didn't want her to be upset. It was her fortieth wedding anniversary tomorrow and this was supposed to be a family

196

Christmas; a chance for them to spend some quality time together. Something his family rarely did. This holiday was supposed to be a celebration. And she was probably right. After all, what other explanation could there be? He'd always known his parents had met in this village, so of course they would've met some of the locals. He'd heard the story several times over the years and knew it by heart. It had always sounded so romantic. That was why he had thought coming back here for their anniversary was such a good idea. It seemed he may have been wrong about that.

His mum was a friend of the then vicar's daughter and was here on holiday for the summer. His dad was passing through the village on a walking holiday and had fallen on Frog Hill, hurting his ankle badly. One of the villagers had taken him in and let him stay until it had healed sufficiently. Leo's mum had a knowledge of herbs and as there was no doctor in the village at the time, she had offered to bind his ankle with a healing recipe she knew. Their eyes had met, they had fallen in love at first sight and a few months later, on December the 23rd, they were married. That was forty years ago.

And it would soon be Leo's fortieth birthday.

He'd always known his mum was pregnant when his parents married. Perhaps this woman, Hettie had spread rumours about them around the village. Perhaps that was why his mum was so upset.

Damn. Why hadn't he thought this through? He assumed bringing them back to the village where they met and fell in love would be a lovely surprise. A way to relive their romance. To walk along the beach they'd once strolled along, hand in hand. To see the places they had stayed. To do the things they'd done so many years ago. But clearly he'd been wrong. Very, very wrong.

Perhaps his mum was right. Perhaps it would be better if they left. He'd have a word with Mia about it later. He didn't care about the money. He was simply unhappy that he'd ruined his parents wedding anniversary tomorrow, and possibly, their Christmas.

'Okay, Mum. I promise. I won't go near the woman. And I'll speak to Mia. If you and Dad and Hal would rather leave, we can go back to London first thing tomorrow. I'll find somewhere fabulous for us all to stay as my way of saying sorry.'

She smiled at him and took his hands in hers. 'There's no need, darling. Let's go back to ours for Christmas. We can stock up on the way, or get someone to deliver. It isn't Christmas Day until Tuesday, so we still have time to prepare. I know you meant well, Leo and I do appreciate the thought. We both do. But you're so much like your father. A true romantic, and sometimes, romance doesn't go quite as one expects. Let's go inside and start packing.'

'I'll be in later, Mum. There's someone I want to see before I go.'

'Leo, darling! You promised.'

'Not the old woman, Mum. It's someone else. And I need to see Mia and explain.'

Elizabeth hesitated. 'Oh well, darling. If you must. But I'd like to leave bright and early, so no going to the pub. If you are stopped for drink driving that will really round things off.'

He smiled and walked away, heading towards Corner Cottage. Why he felt he wanted to see Cathy and say goodbye, he had no idea, and yet he felt he should. No, not that he should. It was that he wanted to. Which was ridiculous, considering they had only met today.

But then again, his mum and dad had fallen in love at first sight and they'd been married forty years.

Is that what had happened to him today? Had he fallen in love at first sight? The little girls had both tugged at his heart strings, there was no doubt about that, especially the older one. There was a sadness about her. And when he'd first turned around in the queue and looked into Cathy's eyes, something deep inside him had definitely stirred. Or perhaps awakened might be a better way to describe the way he'd felt. He'd had several relationships in his life, but none of them had made him feel the way he had when he looked at Cathy. It was as if his entire future had flashed before his eyes. A future that was bright and cheerful, full of love and happiness.

Didn't people say that was what happened when you were drowning? You saw your entire life in a moment. Falling in love was like falling into an ocean, wasn't it? Uncharted waters of love and passion and desire. In that split second, when he'd looked into her eyes, he'd felt all those things. And more.

And his mum had just said, he was so much like his father.

He was a true romantic.

Chapter Twenty-Five

Cathy watched the expression on Daisy's face as the reindeer and the sleigh pulled up outside Corner Cottage. She had never seen her daughter so excited, or Christy's daughter, Dylan, come to that. Their eyes were alight with pure, innocent joy, their hands clasped together as they screamed in delight, and when they were allowed, not just to pet the reindeer, but to each give the reindeer a carrot, they were simply over the moon.

'Mummy, mummy. Did you see me?'

Daisy jumped up and down with joy and Dylan attempted to copy her, losing her balance and tumbling onto her back, giggling at the top of her voice as Daisy tried to pull her up. Christy stepped in to take over.

'Yes, darling. I saw you. You were both very brave girls.'

'And Father Christmas said that we can go for a ride in the sleigh if we are very good. We will be very good, Mummy.'

'I know you will, darling. You're always a good girl. That was very kind of Father Christmas, especially as he'll be so busy this weekend. He's got to make sure all the presents are ready to be delivered on Monday night.'

'This Monday is Christmas Eve?'

'Yes darling. Christmas Day is only three sleeps away.'

'And what do you want for Christmas, Daisy?' a male voice enquired.

Cathy turned around to see the nice man from the queue at the bakery this morning who had said his name was Leo.

'Weindeer,' Dylan shouted, giggling and dancing as best she could in the deep snow.

'Yes,' Daisy said, nodding. 'Reindeer would be lovely. But we don't have a garden, so it wouldn't be fair. And we're not allowed pets, are we Mummy?'

'No, darling,' Cathy quickly said.

'So what would you like other than a reindeer?' Leo asked.

'A doll,' Daisy said, and Dylan nodded. 'Some ballet shoes. But I don't go to ballet now.' She looked extremely sad, and Cathy quickly changed the subject.

'And books, darling. You want lots of books, don't you?'

'Yes. Lots and lots of books. I like reading. Do you like reading?'

'Very much,' Leo replied. 'And what does Mummy want for Christmas?' He smiled at Daisy before looking into Cathy's eyes.

She knew she was blushing but she couldn't help herself and she blushed even more when Daisy replied, 'S-e-x. Mummy wants s-e-x for Christmas.'

For a split second Leo looked shocked and then it was obvious he was trying desperately hard to stop himself from laughing. Christy didn't bother. She shook with laughter.

'Oh Daisy,' Christy said, almost choking. 'You're a treasure. An absolute delight.'

'I don't,' Cathy said, trying to avoid looking at Leo's face. 'And I can explain.'

'There's no need to explain to me,' he said, his voice catching with every word. 'And it's none of my business, but is there anyone in particular you would like to receive this present from?'

'Absolutely not. No. No one. No one at all.'

'Stop digging,' Christy teased, nudging Cathy's arm. 'What my friend means is that she's not seeing anyone at the moment. But if she was seeing someone she would like them to give her that particular present.'

'No I don't. I wouldn't. I definitely don't want that for Christmas.'

Leo raised his brows. 'Well,' he replied, grinning mischievously. 'Now that we've established exactly what you don't want, may I ask if you would like a drink? And your friend and the children, of course.'

'Oh. Um.'

'Yes,' Christy said. 'We'd all like that very much. I hear there's a buffet in the pub.'

'Yes,' he said, smiling at Cathy. 'I heard that too. Shall we see if we can get a seat before it becomes too packed? I think everyone watching and involved with this procession will be in the pub later.'

'Good idea,' Christy said.

'Um.' Cathy hesitated.

'Come on, Cathy. It's Christmas. Remember what I said.' Christy winked and then bent down and lifted Dylan into her arms.

Cathy took Daisy's hand and hoped she wasn't blushing as much as she thought. It felt as if her cheeks were on fire.

'Would you like me to give Daisy a piggyback?' Leo asked. 'The snow's quite deep and she's probably a little too grown-up for you to lift her.'

Cathy glanced from him to Christy and then to Daisy, who was nodding enthusiastically.

'For a little way,' Cathy said.

Leo seemed nice, but she didn't know him from Adam, even though every time he looked at her something inside her felt warm and safe and happy.

He bent down and swung Daisy onto his back with ease. 'Hold tight,' he said. 'We may need to gallop.' He picked up speed, ran a few feet ahead, kicking up snow as they went, and just as Cathy was about to panic, he turned and ran back again, Daisy shrieking with laughter in his ear.

'Mummy go,' Dylan said, trying to clamber over Christy's shoulder and copy what was happening to Daisy.

Christy threw Leo a reprimanding look. 'Thanks,' she said, but she was grinning. 'Come on then.' She shifted Dylan onto her back, and jogged a little way ahead.

'You're very good with children,' Cathy said, still trying to avoid looking at Leo's intense green eyes. 'Do you have children of your own?'

He shook his head. 'No. I'm not married.'

'Nor am I,' Cathy replied, although she had no idea why she said that.

'I've never been married.' Leo was staring at her.

She smiled up at Daisy and tied Daisy's scarf a little tighter. 'Not the marrying kind?'

'No. I am the marrying kind. I've just never met someone I wanted to marry.'

'I bet you've had plenty to choose from though.' Now she did look at him.

He frowned. 'A few, perhaps. What about you? Have you met anyone since your husband passed away?'

She didn't reply immediately. What could she say? She didn't want to lie. And yet…

'No. No one I wanted to marry,' she eventually said.

'Can we go fast again, please?' Daisy asked.

'Absolutely,' Leo said. He smiled at Cathy before trotting ahead, sending showers of snow in his wake.

Chapter Twenty-Six

Jenny watched the procession and smiled all the way through it. Which surprised her rather a lot. She had never been a fan of Christmas, and could take or leave all the decorations, and yet since the supper party at Jet's, she had been feeling decidedly festive. So much so, she had put up decorations in the bakery and also in the cottage and she had been working on a new recipe for different varieties of shortbread. She had even made a Christmas cake for herself. A large Christmas cake. What she was going to do with it, she had no idea. Put it in the bakery, for sale, perhaps. Along with the Christmas pudding she had also made for herself, with extra cherries and oranges with a whiskey and marmalade centre. It was full of walnuts, hazelnuts, almonds and pecans, and again was definitely on the large side. It was as if she was preparing food for a Christmas she wouldn't be having. A family Christmas. A

Christmas surrounded by love and laughter, friendship and warmth.

She had planned to go home after seeing the reindeer and the sleigh, and yet she found herself trudging through the snow across the green towards The Frog and Lily. The place was already heaving, by the cacophony of voices she could hear emanating from that direction. Poor Toby, Freda and Alec would be rushed off their feet. The carollers hadn't even arrived yet, and when they did, there would be no room to move.

'Hey Jenny!' A female voice called from somewhere close by, and as she peered across the lane which was brightly lit by lamplight and the multi-coloured lights between, she spotted Cathy, who she recognised from seeing her in the bakery.

Jenny dashed across the lane and smiled. 'Hello Cathy. Where's Christy and the children?'

Cathy nodded ahead of her, and Jenny saw the tall, blond man from this morning who had insisted on paying for Cathy and Christy's cakes, and also for Mia and Ella's. He appeared to have Daisy on his back, and ahead of him was Christy with Dylan.

'They seem to be enjoying themselves,' Jenny said. 'Did you know him before today?'

Cathy shook her head. 'No. He started talking to us and the children in the queue.'

Jenny pulled a face. 'If he wasn't such a nice man, I'd be worried that that was a bit weird.'

'I know. That thought struck me. As a mother, you're always wary of strangers, especially when you've—' She stopped abruptly and glanced at Jenny before continuing: 'When you've seen what can happen. But sometimes you just get a feeling about someone, if you know what I mean. And you simply know the person is one of the nicest men you've ever met.'

'I know exactly what you mean. Can you keep a secret?'

Cathy furrowed her brows before smiling warmly. 'Yes. I can definitely keep a secret.'

Jenny smiled. 'I'm telling you this because you're only here for the holidays and when it all goes wrong, I won't have to feel humiliated by seeing you and knowing that you know.'

'That sounds complicated.'

'Love is, isn't it?'

Cathy stiffened. 'It shouldn't be. I think sometimes it's us who makes it complicated. We want someone we can't have. Or we don't want someone who wants us. I take it you're in love with someone?'

Jenny let out a long, sad sigh. 'I was. I lived in Florence until a few weeks ago, but I discovered my boyfriend in bed with the girl I thought was my best friend. It broke my heart completely. I hadn't just lost a boyfriend, I'd lost my best friend too.'

'God. That's awful.'

'My cousin Justin owns the bakery here, but he's now a Hollywood star. Although that's another story. To cut a long story short, I asked if I could come and live in his cottage and take over the bakery. I was actually running away. I thought it would take me years to get over what Silvio my boyfriend, and Bianca my best friend, did. And yet the odd thing is, I've met someone. Someone I would never dream of having a relationship with in the normal course of events. But the minute I saw him I felt something. Something deep within me. And every time I've seen him since, I look forward to the next time that I'll see him. Does that make any sense at all?'

'It makes complete sense. Do you think he feels the same about you?'

Jenny shook her head. 'I think he likes me. I think he likes me a lot. But he's such a lovely guy, he could simply be being friendly. He's nice to everyone he meets. He cares about people. How do I know if he feels more for me than friendship? He did offer to make dinner for me once, but I made an excuse and refused.'

'There's only one way to find out. Ask him to dinner. Or out for coffee, or a drink.'

'It sounds so easy. But it isn't, is it? I'm scared of getting hurt again. I'm scared to trust my feelings. I'm telling a complete stranger about my love life.'

Cathy grinned at her. 'I'm not a complete stranger. I've been in the bakery a few times. And if it makes you feel any better, I'll tell you a secret too. I've met someone, and he makes me feel exactly the same as you say your man makes you feel.'

Jenny opened her eyes wide and pulled a face. 'It's not the same man, is it? That would be too awful.'

'I hadn't thought of that. What colour hair does your man have?'

'Blond,' Jenny said.

Cathy's gaze shot forward and she sounded panicked. 'So does Leo.'

'Leo?' Jenny nodded towards Leo and Daisy still several yards ahead. 'Phew. Mine's, Glen.'

'The vicar?' Cathy queried. 'Gosh. That's a relief.' She suddenly smiled. 'Have you heard about the Wishing Tree?'

Jenny nodded. 'Yes. Hettie told me all about it. Why?'

'Mia told me. And I was just wondering. There's no harm in making a wish, is there?'

Jenny shrugged. 'I suppose not. But what do we wish for? To find the love of our life, or to find someone who will never lie or cheat or steal, or hurt us in any way?'

'Perhaps we just wish for someone to love us on equal terms. It's Sunday tomorrow. We could go and make a wish. Apparently we must never go there on a Monday.'

'Because of the curse,' Jenny said, nodding. 'I'm up for that tomorrow. What about your friend? Is she in love with someone?'

Cathy shook her head. 'Not as far as I know. But this village seems to have a lot of very handsome men.' She grinned. 'And we're here until the 2nd of January.'

'I think he's waiting for you,' Jenny said, nodding her head in Leo's direction. 'I'll leave you to it.'

'No,' said Cathy. 'Join us. Unless you're meeting someone else.'

'I'm not. And I would love to join you. Thank you. I'm hoping for a chance to have a friendly chat with Glen this evening, and I would have felt a bit sad propping up the bar alone.'

'I'm not sure anyone would be alone here,' Cathy said. 'Everyone I've met seems very friendly.'

'That's one of the reasons I wanted to come,' Jenny said. 'Justin was always telling me that no one could ever be miserable or alone in Little Pondale. And I was definitely feeling both those things in Florence.'

Chapter Twenty-Seven

By the time the carollers and everyone else in the procession piled into The Frog and Lily, there was definitely no room to move and although the buffet had been laid out in the function room, that was small, and also getting full. Mia and Jet had only planned to pop in for one quick drink because they didn't want to leave the reindeer standing outside in the snow and Little M was getting more excitable than usual.

'Make room for Father Christmas and his wife,' someone shouted when Hettie and Fred arrived, and despite the number of people, the crowds parted like the Red Sea, letting Hettie, Fred, Mia, Jet and Little M get to the bar.

'I've never seen it this busy in here, deary,' Hettie said, as Toby served them.

'It's crazy,' he replied. 'Especially as we're one down. I know I shouldn't mention her, but my sister was a brilliant worker.'

'She was, deary. I agree. It's just a pity she was also a bit of a bad lot. At least Freda and Alec haven't gone away.'

'Not yet. But they're hoping to get a last-minute flight, or at least Mum is, and Dad won't let her go alone. God knows what I'll do then.'

'Can't you get some staff?' Mia asked.

Toby shrugged. 'I think they've tried. Good staff are hard to come by. I'll see you later. Who's next?'

'May I have three glasses of mulled wine, two glasses of orange juice, and a pint of your best bitter, please?' Leo was standing beside Mia, and she turned around to face him.

'Hello,' she said, moving over slightly as Ella and Gill and Lori and Franklin came to join them.

'Hello,' he replied, before the smile drained from his face.

Mia turned and saw that Hettie was staring at him yet again.

'I believe you know my mother,' Leo said, to everyone's surprise.

'I do, deary,' Hettie replied, above the din of jovial voices, some of whom were still singing carols. 'I knew your father, too.'

'And you think I look like someone else? Someone called Hector?'

'You do, deary. Very much in fact.'

'And he is, whom, exactly?'

'He was my husband, but he's dead now, deary.'

214

'I'm sorry for your loss.' Leo paid for the drinks that Toby had put on a tray for him and was about to walk away, when Hettie's words stopped him in his tracks.

'I'm sorry for your loss too, deary.'

'My loss? I don't know what you mean. I haven't lost anyone.'

'Is that what your mother tells you, deary? Because that's not the truth.'

'Oh? And what exactly is the truth?'

'Perhaps you should ask your mother.'

'I'm asking you. You appear to be the one who seems to have something to say.'

'I've got a lot to say, deary, but I'm not sure if you'd want to hear it.'

Leo seemed to hesitate for just a second before he smiled and tipped his head in her direction.

'I don't think I do. And we're leaving first thing in the morning.'

'You're leaving?' This was the first Mia had heard of it.

'You're leaving?' Cathy repeated Mia's question, and she looked equally as surprised and concerned.

Leo put the tray back on the bar and turned to Cathy. 'I was going to tell you later. I'm sorry.' He glanced at Mia. 'And you, Mia. I apologise, and naturally, we're not looking for a refund. This simply isn't the right place for us to spend our holiday. I'll return the keys tomorrow.'

215

'Okay,' Mia said. 'If you're sure that's what you want.'

He glanced again at Cathy, who was still standing, staring at him. 'It's not what I want. But I'm outnumbered. And this is a family holiday, after all.'

'So she's running away, is she, deary?' Hettie said. 'Just like she did forty years ago.'

'Excuse me?' Leo glared at Hettie. 'If you're referring to my mother, she's not running away. She simply doesn't like it here. She's a city girl at heart.'

'Is she now? She wasn't forty years ago.'

He hesitated again, but as Cathy suddenly turned away, he hurried after her.

'Your drinks,' Toby called after him, but he had disappeared into the crowd.

'Okay, Hettie,' Mia said. 'What was all that about?'

Hettie stared into the crowd and shook her head. 'It was about a woman telling lies. He needs to know the truth, but I don't know if I have the heart to tell him.'

'Who?' Jet asked. 'Leo?'

Hettie nodded.

'What truth?' Mia said.

'The truth Elizabeth has obviously kept from him for forty years. The truth of who he really is.'

'What?' Mia darted a look at Jet, who was shaking his head and frowning. 'Who is he then?'

Hettie seemed to awake as if from a trance. 'Well, isn't it obvious? He's the spitting image of his father.'

'No he's not. I've seen his father.'

'No you haven't, deary. Hector's been dead for years.'

'I told you so,' said Lori.

'Are you saying that your husband Hector was Leo Hardman's dad?' Mia asked.

'Yes, deary. That's exactly what I'm saying.'

'Don't look at me,' Fred said. 'The first I heard of it was when we were in the sleigh, after Hettie spotted him. She told me all about it just a while ago. And I'm with Hettie. That young man has a right to know.'

'That Hector Burnstall was his dad?' Mia still couldn't get her head around this revelation. 'But how?'

Hettie tutted. 'Now deary, you of all people should know how these things happen. But I'm not sure that a crowded pub is the best place to discuss it.'

It was a bit late for that, but Mia merely nodded.

'You'll tell us later?'

'Yes, deary. I'll tell you later. But now I think I need a very stiff drink. A very stiff drink indeed.'

Chapter Twenty-Eight

'Cathy! Cathy, please let me explain.' Leo caught up with Cathy just before she reached the table where Jenny, Christy and the children were waiting for their drinks. He reached out to her and grabbed her wrist.

She twisted round and glowered at him, yanking her arm free and virtually snarling when she spoke. 'Don't touch me. I thought you were different. But you're not. You're just like him. You pretend to be nice and then you do this.'

She held her arm up and Leo gasped when he saw the impressions his fingers had left on her skin.

'Oh my God, I'm sorry. I'm so, so sorry. I didn't mean to grab you that hard. I wouldn't dream of hurting you.'

'I've heard that before. And I've been lied to before. It's not going to happen again. Goodbye.'

'But Cathy?'

'Stay away from me. And stay away from Daisy.'

She turned her back on him and he didn't know what to say or do to make things right. He wished he could turn back the clock. Just by a few minutes. To before he went to the bar. Before he saw that woman. Before he said he was leaving. Before Cathy looked at him with fear in her eyes and loathing in her voice.

This was turning into a disaster. How could a Christmas holiday in a cosy, country cottage in a tiny village by the sea, turn into such a nightmare?

He watched Cathy talk to Christy. He saw the look she gave him. He waited while they scooped the children up and cradled them protectively as if they were scared he might hurt them. Then he saw the look that Jenny gave him. A look of contempt. A look of loathing. What had he done to deserve this? He wasn't a guy to be terrified of. To be feared. To be despised. And yet that was the way all three women had looked at him. And now they had all walked out in disgust.

His blood boiled, and his temper grew. He turned and marched back to the bar, and stood before the woman who had ruined his evening.

'I think you owe me an explanation.'

'Oh!' Hettie said, in surprise. 'I thought you'd gone.'

'I haven't.'

'So I see, deary. Are you sure you want to hear this from me, and not your mother?'

'I want to hear your version. And then I'll hear my mother's.'

'Version, deary? I'll tell you the truth.'

Mia interrupted: 'Leo, I think you're understandably cross, but I don't think you should have this conversation here. Apart from the fact that we're almost having to shout over the noise, do you really want details of your private life blurted out in a pub?'

'Mia's right,' Jet said. 'This is neither the time nor the place.'

'I want to hear it! I want to hear what you have to say.' Leo's voice was slightly calmer, although he still felt furious inside. 'No one knows me here. And frankly, I couldn't care less what anyone here thinks.'

Glen suddenly appeared. 'What's going on? I've just seen Cathy outside and she's terribly upset, not to mention Jenny. I offered to walk home with them and they glared at me as if I were the devil himself.'

Leo felt as if he had been punched in the stomach and stabbed in the heart all at once. Cathy was terribly upset. That was the last thing he wanted her to be.

'Could we use the church, Glen?' Mia asked. 'Just for a moment. Hettie has something she needs to tell Leo, and we don't think it should be here in the pub.'

'Of course. I'll open the church up now. Come with me.'

'Come on, Hettie,' Mia said. 'Leo. Come with us. Let's get this over.'

Leo followed Hettie and Fred and Mia, Jet and Glen, with Little M trotting along beside them.

'We won't come in, Leo,' Mia said. 'If you promise us that you won't get cross, or do anything you may regret.'

'Good God. What does everyone take me for? I'm not a violent man. I would never hit a woman, or strike her, or hurt her in any way. All I want is the answer to a simple question. And you can come with us. I don't care.'

They all trundled into the church and sat in the pews at the back.

'Well, deary,' Hettie said. 'There's no point in beating around the bush, so I'll come straight out with it. Your mother, Elizabeth was staying in this village with the daughter of the vicar at the time. Hector and I had been married for fifteen years, and despite wanting a child, it wasn't to be. I reacted badly when I was told it would never happen, and God forgive me, I turned away from Hector. Elizabeth was young and very, very beautiful. And even though Hector was twenty years her senior, he was an extremely handsome man in those days. Just like you are, deary. I won't say your mother was to blame, but Hector strayed. Elizabeth told him she was with child a few weeks later, and in a state of utter shame and guilt and desperation, Hector told me about the baby. Together, we agreed that if Elizabeth were willing, we would adopt the child. She had no parents, and no one to help her, and it seemed the best solution for us all. And then your father, or the man you call your father, was walking on Frog Hill and fell and hurt his ankle. One of the villagers, Mrs Dunlop, took him in, and that very day, Elizabeth met him. She had skills with healing herbs and potions and she dressed Alistair's ankle. A few weeks later, they were both gone, and we never heard from Elizabeth again. We would've tried to trace her, and your father, but he hadn't told anyone where he came from and no one had thought to ask. We didn't even know his surname. As for your mother, I think it best if she tells you exactly what her background is, but suffice to say, she hadn't given the vicar or his daughter her real surname. She was an orphan, that's all we knew, and she had come to the village with a fortune-teller, for the Summer Fête. She got friendly with the vicar's daughter and stayed on for the summer. That's it, deary. That's the truth. My dear, departed husband Hector was your father.'

Leo hadn't said a word, and even now, he didn't. He merely looked at Hettie's face as if he were in some kind of trance.

'Leo?' Jet asked. 'Are you okay?'

He glanced at Jet and nodded. 'So my dad is not my dad, and my brother is only my half-brother, and my mum was an orphan, and a traveller, I think they're called. So basically, everything in my life is a lie. And I'm not as surprised as I should be. It's as if, somehow, I've always known that things weren't what they seemed.'

'Yes, deary, Hettie said. 'And your real dad is dead and has just passed on to his new life. It's such a shame you weren't here sooner, or you could have met him. In spirit, of course.'

'Hettie,' Jet interrupted. 'I don't think Leo needs to hear about that. He's got quite enough to think about.'

'What was he like?' Leo asked.

Hettie smiled. 'He was a lovely man. Kind, considerate and caring. He never forgave himself for what he did and he always hoped that one day, he would meet you, but to tell you the truth, deary, I never thought we ever would. I was certain Elizabeth would never come back here.'

Leo let out a little laugh. 'She wouldn't have, if it hadn't been for me. I arranged this as an anniversary surprise. Little did I know that I would be the one getting the surprise. The surprise of my life. More than one in fact. I meet a woman and fall in love. And I find out I'm not the man I thought I was.' He got to his feet and walked towards the door, turning as he opened it. 'Thank you, Hettie,' he said. 'I don't think this has really sunk in just yet. May I come and see you, sometime in the future? I think I'd like to hear more about Hector, and possibly see some photos, if you have them?'

'You're welcome anytime, deary. Isn't he, Fred?'

Fred nodded. 'Anytime at all.'

Leo nodded and smiled wanly. 'And thank you for not saying anything awful about my mother. I wish I could say that she paid you the same courtesy, but unfortunately she didn't. Good night. Oh, and Merry Christmas everyone.'

'Are you okay?' Jet asked again. 'Do you want me to walk with you?'

Leo let out a snort of laughter. 'Thank you, Jet, but no. I think I can manage from here.'

'Did you say you'd fallen in love?' Mia called after him. 'With Cathy, I assume?'

Leo turned and gave her another wane smile. 'For all the good it'll do me.' And he closed the door behind him and trudged through the snow to Sunbeam Cottage.

This was going to be unpleasant, but it had to be done. He had to ask his mum. He had to see if, after all these years, she would finally tell him the truth. A truth that explained so much. About why, although he knew his mum and dad loved him, they never loved him quite as much as they loved Hal.

He realised now, that he had spent his entire life trying to please his mum. He was almost forty and he was still doing it. This trip to Little Pondale had been an attempt to please her, and his dad. Or the man he had believed to be his dad. Well, this had blown up in his face. But perhaps it was for the best. Now that he knew for certain. And he did know. He believed every word that Hettie had said.

'There you are, darling,' Elizabeth said as he opened the door of Sunbeam Cottage and walked into the living room. She paled visibly as her eyes met his. 'You've spoken to that evil woman, haven't you? Even though I begged you not to.'

'What's going on?' Hal asked. 'Leo, what's up with you? You look as if you've seen a ghost.'

'No,' Leo said. 'But I do want to hear the truth.'

'What truth?' Elizabeth turned away and busied herself filling everyone's glasses. 'That woman is a liar.'

Alistair sighed and got to his feet. 'He knows, darling, and I've known since before he was born. Perhaps it's for the best. It's time to stop lying to ourselves and to everyone else.'

Elizabeth cast horror-stricken eyes to her husband's face. 'You knew? For all these years, you knew?'

Alistair nodded. 'Apart from the fact that he looks nothing like me and, over the years, we've never had any interests or hobbies in common, I'm pretty good at maths. You led me to believe he was premature, and yet the midwife made it clear from things she said, that he wasn't. It was obvious you fell pregnant weeks before I had my fall on Frog Hill.'

'I can explain,' Elizabeth said, her voice cracking, her eyes desperate.

'There's no need to explain anything to me,' Alistair said. 'I loved you then. I love you now.' He looked at Leo and smiled. 'And I love you too, Leo, although perhaps I haven't been the best father to you that I could have been.'

Leo shrugged. 'There's no need to explain anything to me either. I think I've heard all I need to hear.'

'Well, I sure as hell haven't,' Hal said, his confused gaze darting from Leo, to Elizabeth to Alistair and back to Leo. 'Perhaps someone would like to explain to me what in God's name is going on.'

Chapter Twenty-Nine

Cathy couldn't believe it. Why was she so annoyed? Why had she stormed out like that?

It wasn't as if Leo owed her anything. It wasn't as if they had been dating. All he was – or what she had thought he was – was a nice man who had spent some time with her and her daughter. Just because he was leaving far sooner than she expected and because there seemed to be some drama going on in his life, it shouldn't have affected her. And yet it had. And when he had grabbed her wrist, she had instinctively reacted. That wasn't his fault, that was her natural instinct kicking in. She had sworn to herself that no man was ever going to hurt or try to control her again.

And she knew Leo hadn't hurt her intentionally. He hadn't meant to grab her wrist so hard. Somehow she knew, deep down inside that Leo wasn't the sort of man to harm a woman, and certainly not in a fit of anger. He wasn't like Keith.

He was probably the complete opposite, in fact. Everything he'd done so far had been.

But it was too late now, and anyway, the man was leaving in the morning. And she'd known him for precisely one day. Not even a day.

So why was she experiencing such strange emotions? Why did her stomach feel as if it had turned into a washing machine, tumbling back and forth and spinning her insides around? Why did it feel as if her heart had, yet again, been broken?

It was ludicrous. Completely ridiculous.

But the look of hurt and pain and sadness she'd seen in Leo's incredibly intense green eyes, had been very real. And there had been something else in his eyes. Something she had seen in a man's eyes before. Something she had seen in her husband's eyes, just before he died.

It was the look of loss, of promise, of love – a love that could no longer be.

And that look had been in Leo's eyes as she had turned and walked away.

Now her head was telling her it couldn't possibly be the case.

But her heart was telling her it was so.

Her heart was telling her she had fallen in love, probably at first sight. And that the feeling was reciprocated.

Chapter Thirty

The ride home to Little Pond Farm in the sleigh pulled by the reindeer, was magical. At least it would have been had Mia not been mulling over what had happened in the church.

'I still can't believe it,' she said, as she, Jet, Ella, Gill, Lori and Franklin made the journey home. 'I can't believe that Leo is Hector's biological son. Or that Hector had an affair.'

'Neither can I,' said Jet. 'And I really feel for Leo. He'd planned what he thought would be the perfect Christmas get-away and anniversary celebration and it's turned into a complete nightmare for him. I wonder what he's going to say to his mum.'

'More importantly,' Ella said. 'I wonder if his other dad knows. If Mr Hardman knows the truth. That his first-born son is not his son. That's going to go down like a lead balloon if he doesn't.'

'Goodness,' Lori said. 'What a complete and utter mess. I wouldn't want to be Elizabeth right now.'

The bells on the reindeer harness jingled as they trotted through the snow. The evening air was clear and cold, the moon was almost full and the sky was filled with stars. It was a beautiful evening. The perfect evening for romance.

'Did you hear what he said as he left?' Mia glanced at Jet, who was guiding the reindeer and the sleigh as if he had been born to do so.

'About him being in love with Cathy?' Jet smiled at her and nodded.

'I think they only met today but do you know what? I think it was obvious the moment he saw her. And he was so good with those kids. What's more, I could've sworn she felt the same for him. I may be wrong of course, but there was something in the way she looked at him. And I'll tell you what else was odd. She said that her husband has been dead for three years, but Daisy mentioned an uncle Keith and Cathy paled visibly. I got the feeling there was something going on. Something weird. And I think there's more to Cathy's story than meets the eye.'

'Well, it did look as if she had a black eye that first day,' said Lori. 'And if that's the case, perhaps it was this uncle Keith who gave it to her. And he may not be an actual uncle of course. He may be someone she was seeing.'

Jet shook his head. 'And I thought this was going to be a really happy Christmas. It seems that I was wrong. For some people it's going to be anything but.'

Mia nodded. 'But it's definitely going to be a Christmas we'll all remember. And I did promise you that.'

Chapter Thirty-One

Jenny wasn't sure what she should do as she walked up the lane after leaving Corner Cottage. She'd just seen Mia and the others gliding by in the sleigh, no doubt going home to Little Pond Farm. She had waved but they clearly hadn't seen her. They would have stopped if they had. She could go home; or she could do what she had intended and go and talk to Glen in the pub.

'Jenny?' She was surprised to hear her name. Especially as she immediately recognised the voice.

'Glen?'

'Hello,' he said, walking down the drive of Hettie and Fred's cottage. 'Where are you off to?'

'I'm not completely sure. It's been a very strange night so far. The carols were beautiful, and the reindeer and the sleigh, complete with Father Christmas and his wife, not forgetting those adorable Huskies, were all pretty special, but the night took an unexpected turn.'

'They were, weren't they? And you're right about it being a very strange night. I thought village life would be boring. It seems it couldn't be farther from the truth. I'm beginning to wish I could stay.'

'Could stay?' Had she heard him correctly. 'You mean you're not?'

He shook his head, somewhat sadly she was certain.

'No. It was a temporary position, for which I was thankful when I came. I didn't want to be stuck in a village. But now. Now that I've been told the parish will be merging and this one will effectively close down, meaning I can move on, and to a city parish. Now I find I'm not as pleased to hear that as I thought I'd be.'

'So you're leaving?'

He nodded. 'In the New Year.'

'And nothing can be done to make you stay?'

He met her eyes and several seconds passed between them.

'Do you want me to stay?' Glen finally asked, still looking into her eyes.

She nodded, still looking into his. 'Yes, Glen. I think I do. In fact, I know I do. Is that possible?'

He moved a step closer. 'If you'd asked me that this morning, I'd probably have said no, but now, tonight. I would say anything is possible. Anything at all. I know we haven't known each other long, and I know I'm no great catch, but if I were to ask you on a date, is there a chance you might say yes?'

'There's a very good chance,' Jenny replied. 'In fact, I know I would. But I've been hurt badly, Glen, and I don't want to be hurt again. If you're moving miles away in the very near future, I'm not sure it's a good idea, are you?'

He shook his head as he moved even closer. 'No. It's probably a very bad idea. And yet.'

'And yet?'

'And yet I want to ask you, Jenny. And I want to find a way to stay.'

'And I want to say yes. And I want you to stay, Glen. I really, truly do. I know you won't believe in this, and I know I shouldn't either, but I've heard about a Wishing Tree, and I was going there tomorrow. Perhaps you'd like to come along. I mean, you never know, do you? There's no harm in wishing, is there?'

He shook his head. He was now standing so close she could feel his warm breath on her cheek. 'No harm at all, as far as I can see. Although I shouldn't go there as a vicar, but I could go there as a man. A man who definitely has something to wish for.'

'Then it's a date?' she said, her own breath coming short and sharp.

'Yes, Jenny. It's a date. But I'd really like to kiss you now.'

'I'd like that too,' she said.

'You would?'

She nodded. 'I would, Glen. I definitely would.'

And she did. More than even she expected.

Chapter Thirty-Two

It was stupid. Of course it was. Cathy shrugged on her coat, pulled on her gloves and sat her woolly hat firmly on her head.

'Are we sure about this?' She glanced at Christy who was buttoning up Dylan's duffle coat.

'Yes. We are. We'll go and make our wishes and then I'll put the dinner in the oven and get the kids to help make a trifle. That'll keep them entertained. And we'll wait and see what happens.'

'Ready, Mummy,' Daisy said. 'Are we going to see that nice man today?'

Cathy stiffened. 'No darling. We're going to see a very special tree. The one I told you about this morning. Have you written down your wish?'

Daisy nodded and held out a piece of paper.

'Oh I mustn't look,' said Cathy. 'Give it to Auntie Christy so that you don't lose it.'

Daisy smiled excitedly and handed over her wish. It was folded in two and had a hole with a piece of red ribbon through it, ready to be tied to a branch of the tree.

Cathy checked her own wish was in her pocket and sighed deeply as she did. She hadn't been at all sure what to wish for when they'd written them over breakfast this morning and it had taken her five attempts until she was sure what it was she wanted most. Like Daisy's, her wish was folded in two and had a ribbon running through a little hole.

'Let's go and get Jenny then,' Christy said. 'She did say twelve, last night, didn't she?'

Cathy nodded. 'She did. Come on Daisy and Dylan. Let's go and make our wishes.'

Dylan's wish, which Cathy had, was longer than everyone else's, but then her writing was larger than theirs, and hers was mainly pictures. Cathy and Christy had agreed that they would read each other's child's wish, in case it was something they wanted for Christmas, or something Cathy or Christy could make happen. If it was something farfetched, they would simply say that not all wishes could come true. Dylan's drawings were all of toys, so it was clear what she was wishing for. Cathy and Christy had, thankfully, bought all the ones she'd drawn, along with one or two more, so Dylan would definitely get her wish. But Christy had refused to tell Cathy what it was that Daisy had wished for.

'I'll tell you later,' she had said, and smiled oddly. 'It's not something we can buy, but it's something that, with a lot of luck and a little bit of magic, could definitely come true.'

No matter how much Cathy coaxed her, Christy wouldn't say more.

They walked across the lane, over the village green and rang the bell at Jenny's cottage.

She answered within seconds, already wearing her hat and coat.

'Good morning,' she beamed. 'Isn't it a lovely morning?'

It was. The sky was clear and bright. It was cold, but not too cold that it took your breath away. Just cold enough to make one's breath mist the air, and everyone's cheeks turn red, and to not want to stand around for long.

'You seem very happy this morning,' Cathy said. 'Did something happen last night after you left us?'

Jenny nodded madly, grinning and glancing down at the children's rosy cheeks. 'I'll tell you all about it. I bumped into Glen when I left. He had been with Hettie and Fred. I'm not exactly sure what happened because as a vicar, Glen felt he couldn't tell me, but something went on last night concerning Hettie and also Leo.'

'Leo? I heard him talking to an elderly woman at the bar and neither of them sounded happy. Was that Hettie? The one who was in the sleigh last night?'

Jenny nodded. 'That was Hettie.'

Cathy frowned. 'That's when he said he was leaving today. And when I got annoyed and upset. The vicar didn't say what it was about?'

Jenny shook her head. 'No.' She lowered her voice as they walked. 'But he kissed me and we came back here and ... talked.' She waved her hands around excitedly.

'Talked? Or *talked*?' Christy asked, grinning.

'The second one,' Jenny said, shaking her head and laughing gleefully. 'Don't ask me how because we hadn't intended to. But you know how it is. Candles and wine and music. A roaring fire and twinkling lights. A dark, cold winter's night.'

'Oh yes,' Christy said. 'We know all about those. Although not for a while now. So did you *talk* all night?'

Jenny nodded. 'All night. And this morning too before he had to leave for church.' She burst out laughing.

'Jenny Lake,' Cathy said, laughing. 'You are a bad, bad girl.'

'That's odd.' Jenny winked at her and Christy. 'That's exactly what the vicar said.'

'Um. Girls.' Christy was suddenly serious and she nodded towards Sunbeam Cottage. 'There's no car in the drive.'

'That means he's gone,' Cathy said. 'And he didn't even come to say goodbye. Not that there is any reason why he should have, of course. No reason at all.' She fought back the stupid tear that was prickling at her eye.

'I really thought he would,' Jenny said.

'Me too,' said Christy. 'Men. Who needs them?'

They walked on for a while in silence, save for the giggles from Dylan and Daisy as they jumped and ran and fell in the deep, white snow. When Christy finally spoke, it was on a completely different subject.

'We're going ice skating on the pond this afternoon,' she said. 'Apparently it's safe and lots of people do it. There's another pond up here, near this tree we're going to, and people skate on that one too. Do you want to join us, Jenny?'

Jenny nodded. 'I'd like that very much. Glen was going to come to the tree with us today, but he's going to visit the Bishop instead. He wants to see if there is any way he could make this a permanent post. He doesn't hold out much hope, but anything is worth a try. He may come here to make a wish of his own if he doesn't get any joy with his uncle, even though he doesn't really believe in stuff like this.'

'So he's leaving?' Cathy asked.

'Yes. Unless we can find a way for him to stay.'

'Then it's pretty clear what you'll be wishing for,' Christy said.

Chapter Thirty-Three

'I can't believe it's Christmas Eve,' Mia said, over breakfast the following day. 'Where did Sunday go?'

Jet finished his coffee and smiled. 'I think you and Ella spent most of it wrapping presents, didn't you? Before popping out to visit Hettie, or wherever it was you went. I can't believe it's snowing again. We're definitely going to have a white Christmas.'

Mia grinned at him. 'What a good thing we've got the sleigh. It's so much easier than the car, and much more fun, too. I could get used to having reindeer, couldn't you?'

Jet gave her an odd look. 'Possibly. They're no harder to look after than any other animal. They're cute and they could be an added draw, on the customer front. Especially at this time of year.'

'You mean you might consider it?' She raised her brows at him over the rim of her coffee cup.

'I'm considering a lot of things,' he said, getting up and kissing her on her cheek.

'Oh? That sounds interesting.'

'It is. But now I've got to go and help milk the cows.'

'I'd come and help, but I have mince pies to make, and cook books to read.' Mia smiled at him and he glanced around the kitchen, sighing dramatically. 'What was that for?' she asked.

'I'm simply trying to remember it as it is now before it turns into a war zone later.'

Mia slapped him on the arm. 'Oh ye of little faith. You might be surprised.'

'And so might you,' he said, winking and grinning at her as he strolled out the kitchen door with Little M scampering after him, her claws clicking across the tiled floor.

'What did he mean by that?' Mia asked Ella as Ella came into the kitchen.

'Who?'

'Jet, of course.'

'Oh. What did he say?'

Mia tutted. 'He said I might be surprised by something.'

'Perhaps he's getting you something special for Christmas and it'll surprise you. Have you made coffee?'

'Yes. It's in the pot here on the table. Perhaps he has, but it sounded odd.'

Ella poured herself a mug of coffee and sat beside Mia, leaning her elbows on the kitchen table. 'Well, you'll find out tomorrow, won't you? What are you doing today?'

'I'm cooking, and so are you. Gill and Mum are helping too.'

'Oh joy,' Ella said, yawning dramatically. 'I thought this was the season to be jolly.'

'It is.'

'Then why are we cooking?' Ella gulped her coffee and sighed as if she had really needed it.

'Because it's about time we learnt how to. We're in our mid-thirties, Ella. We should know how to stuff a turkey, and make perfect roast potatoes.'

'I do know how to make perfect roast potatoes. You open a bag of frozen ones and stick them in the oven.'

Mia sighed. 'From scratch, I meant.'

'Why would we want to do that?' Ella frowned at her.

'Because we do. Because it's Christmas. We're going to make golden roast potatoes with butter, sage and rosemary, delicious Brussels sprouts with pancetta and chestnuts, and honey glazed carrots. Oh, and cranberry sauce. From fresh cranberries. To name but a few of the delights we'll be making today.'

That was clearly a shock to Ella. 'Fresh cranberries? We don't have to go and pick them, do we?'

Mia laughed. 'No. Mum bought them from the supermarket the other day.'

'Thank God for that,' Ella said, looking genuinely relieved. 'So are we only having vegetables for Christmas dinner? You haven't mentioned those little sausages wrapped in bacon, or the turkey. If this is a trial run today, shouldn't we also do those?'

'We're preparing those too. I didn't want to bombard you with too many things at once. I know you scare easily when it comes to cooking.' Mia grinned at her. 'Seriously though, Ella. I want to do this properly. I want this year to be really special. To be magical.'

'Then I hope that's what you wished for at the Wishing Tree yesterday afternoon.'

Mia laughed and nodded. 'I also asked Glen to pray for me. I need all the positive divine intervention I can get.'

Ella grinned. 'Good luck with that. I was surprised to see Glen there, weren't you?' She helped herself to a slice of toast from the rack on the table and spread it thickly with butter and marmalade. 'I didn't think he believed in the Wishing Tree.'

'Yes. Especially when he told us why. I'm so pleased he and Jenny have got together.'

'Ah, but the Bishop's about to tear them apart. Didn't you hear what Glen said. He'd been to see his uncle who told him that it would cost far too much to keep this as a separate parish, as much as he and the diocese would like to. So Glen will leave here early next year.' Ella bit into her toast.

244

Mia's smile grew bigger and she topped up her coffee and Ella's too. 'Oh no he won't. I'm seeing to that this morning. I discussed it with Jet last night and he agreed. This village needs a church and a vicar. It wouldn't be the same without it.'

'But hardly anyone goes to church these days and the place is falling down.'

'Which is why I'm going to take a leaf out of Mattie's book and make a little donation. Well, a big donation actually, but only on one condition – that Glen stays on as vicar of St Michael and All Angels for the foreseeable future.'

Ella was astonished. 'You can't do that. That's tantamount to blackmail. Or bribery, or something.'

'It's called business, I believe, and I'm doing it, no matter what. I'm going to see Glen today and to sit with him while he calls his uncle. If I'd known about this yesterday morning, I would've gone with him on his visit. It's not the same doing things like this over the telephone. But I've got a feeling, the Bishop will agree.'

Chapter Thirty-Four

'The children are so excited,' Cathy said, as Jenny put several mince pies in a box. 'They're always hyper on Christmas Eve, of course, but this year it's completely different. They loved ice skating yesterday and today we're going tobogganing on Frog Hill. They don't usually get to do things like this, and they've never had snow at Christmas before. It's adding to the magic. What are your plans for Christmas Day? You're welcome to come and join us.'

Jenny smiled. 'That's really kind, but Mia's asked me and Glen to dinner. We'd love to pop in sometime though. I've got a little present for each of the girls.'

'You shouldn't have done that. But please feel free to drop in anytime. We'll be having dinner around two. So either before or after is fine.'

'Great.' Jenny tied the box of mince pies with a Christmas ribbon and grinned as she handed it over the counter. 'I don't know what's come over me. I'm getting more festive by the day. I blame Mia and Jet. Are you doing anything tonight? Glen and I are going to The Frog and Lily and then coming back here for supper. He's doing midnight mass, of course, so I'll be going to church for that.'

Cathy took the box and smiled. 'This entire village is festive. I've never seen anywhere like it. The girls will be manic all evening, waiting for Father Christmas, and Christy and I will be preparing everything for tomorrow, but we may pop into the pub for one quick drink. Just to savour the atmosphere. We won't make midnight mass though. The kids are far too young to stay awake for that. Jenny? Is something wrong?' Jenny's mouth had fallen open and she was staring at Cathy in a peculiar fashion.

Or was she?

Cathy spun around and couldn't believe her eyes.

It was him.

It was Leo.

He was standing outside the bakery, looking in.

At her.

Cathy's eyes shot back towards Jenny. 'It's him, isn't it? I'm not imagining things, am I?'

Jenny shook her head. 'You're not imagining things. It's Leo. Are you okay?'

Cathy nodded. 'I'm fine. I think.'

And then the door opened and Leo came in, briefly nodding his head at Jenny as he said hello, before turning his full attention towards Cathy.

'Hello, Cathy. I know I'm probably the last man on Earth you want to see right now, but please let me explain. Let me apologise. Let me tell you how I feel.'

Cathy turned to face him, and although she hadn't meant to, she could feel herself smiling. She was so pleased to see him. 'You don't need to explain.'

His eyes scanned her face and his frown turned into a smile. 'Don't I?'

'No. Unless you really want to.'

He nodded. 'I really want to, Cathy.'

'I thought you'd left.' She met his eyes and tried to keep her voice calm.

'I had. I took Mum, Dad and Hal home and spent the day with them. It was Mum and Dad's anniversary, after all. I came back first thing this morning and went to see Mia to ask if I might stay on at Sunbeam Cottage, as I'd originally booked it till the New Year.'

'You've all returned?' Cathy couldn't quite believe it. What on earth was going on?

He shook his head and smiled but his expressive eyes held a hint of sadness. 'Just me.'

'Why? Don't you want to spend Christmas with your family?'

He nodded again, not taking his eyes from her face. 'Yes. I very much want to spend Christmas with my family. That's why I came back.'

'What are you saying?' Her breath caught in her throat and her heart skipped a beat.

'I'm saying that I'm hoping my family is here. My new family. The woman I fell head over heels in love with in less than a minute, and the daughter who's already in my heart. I'm saying that I love you, Cathy, and I don't even know your surname, but it doesn't matter. I'm asking if you feel the same. I thought for a moment you did. And then I thought you hated me. But, as silly as this sounds, before we left yesterday morning, I went to a place called the Wishing Tree, and I had the strangest feeling while I was there. It was as if something was telling me not to give up hope. To take a leap of faith. I couldn't get that thought out of my head all day, or last night. I knew this morning that I had to come back. Was I wrong?'

Cathy slowly shook her head and her heart thumped against her chest as if it wanted to burst out. 'No, Leo. You were right. But there are a few things you need to know.'

He beamed at her. 'I've got a lifetime to find out. There's only one thing I need to know right now. Do you feel the same as I do, Cathy?'

He held out both his hands to her, his palms facing up, and she stepped closer, placing her hands in his. His fingers gently closed around hers and it was as if an invisible cloak had suddenly wrapped around her body. She felt safe and warm and more in love than she had ever been before, apart from when she had looked at Daisy moments after giving birth.

'Yes, Leo. I do. I love you. And as incredible as this is, I know that Daisy does too. Christy told me this morning that you're what Daisy wished for. She wished for the nice man called Leo to fall in love with Mummy and to be her new dad.'

Cathy had completely forgotten where she was and it seemed that Leo had too, until Jenny clapped and cheered and shouted. 'Well, kiss her then, Leo!'

And after blinking a couple of times as if realising where he was, that's exactly what Leo did.

When he finally released her and they eventually left the bakery and walked back towards Corner Cottage, hand in hand, Cathy frowned.

'There is something I must tell you, Leo. And I want you to let me tell you it all before you say anything.'

'Okay.' Leo smiled reassuringly. 'But it won't change anything.'

Cathy smiled and sighed deeply. 'It's about a friend of my husband's. His name is Keith and he spent a lot of time with us after my husband died. He blamed himself because he was driving the car when a lorry crashed into the side of them. Keith was only slightly hurt but my husband took the full impact and had life-threatening injuries. They operated and things seemed hopeful, at first, but there were 'complications', the doctor said. I saw the way my husband looked at me when they rushed him back in for another operation. He knew he was going to die, and there was nothing anyone could do. The accident wasn't Keith's fault, but he has what they call, survivor's guilt, I think. He visited us frequently and even came to stay once or twice. But he started drinking heavily and became very controlling. He behaved as if we were in a relationship – which we weren't, and as if Daisy was his daughter. And recently, he began to lose his temper. He's a police officer and he started checking up on me, tracking where I went and what I did. Asking me questions and going through my bag. The final straw came when he said we should spend this Christmas together as a family. I said no and he got mad. He knocked things off a shelf and one of the ornaments hit me just below my eye.'

Leo stiffened noticeably. 'Jesus, Cathy!'

'I was okay,' Cathy continued before Leo could say more. 'He didn't mean it and he was sorry, but it frightened me. He frightened me. I knew I had to get away from him. My grandad died two months ago and he left me some money. It's not a fortune, but it's enough to give me and Daisy a new start. Life has been tough for the last few years and money had been tight. I wanted this to be a special Christmas, so Christy and I found this place. I didn't tell Keith about it but I posted a Christmas card to him, the morning we left, with a note inside telling him we'd gone away and asking him not to try to find us. I told him we needed space. I said that he frightened me and that I didn't want him around Daisy until he got some help. I also told him, once again, that he and I didn't have a future together, regardless of whether or not he sorted himself out. That I thought of him as a friend, but would never feel anything more. I'm not sure if I was cruel, but I had to be honest with him. Christy and I came here, without his knowledge. I'm not sure what he'll do, or how he'll react. I thought that you should know.' She shrugged as she looked into his eyes, and gave a little laugh. 'I come with very little money, but a lot of baggage.'

Leo wrapped her in his arms and kissed her.

'I'm glad you told me,' he said, when he finally eased away. 'And we'll deal with it together. I've got some high-ranking contacts in the police, thanks to my dad and his golf buddies, and if Keith won't seek help himself, I'm sure someone will ensure he gets whatever assistance he needs. You only have to say the word and we'll get things rolling. But whatever happens, you don't have to worry about him again. I can promise you that. I'll make sure you and Daisy are safe. And Christy and Dylan too.' He smiled and kissed her on the tip of her nose. 'And we all come with baggage. As for money, well, that's something else you'll never need to worry about again.'

Cathy looked into his eyes and could see he was sincere. She could also see how much he loved her and as crazy as it seemed, she knew she loved him just as much. And that this would last a lifetime.

Chapter Thirty-Five

Christmas Eve was one of those nights when the universe shows its true beauty. The moon was full, there wasn't a cloud in the sky and even with the glow of street lights and Christmas lights, millions of stars twinkled across the heavens. It had snowed on and off all day and the blanket of white sparkled beneath the festive lights and the silvery glow from the moon.

At precisely five p.m. the snow had finally stopped. It was perfect timing because Fred and Hettie had reprised their roles of Father and Mrs Christmas. While Mia, Jet and the others, sat in front of the roaring fire in The Frog and Lily, drinking mulled wine and singing Christmas songs with the locals, Hettie and Fred took the children in the village, including Daisy and Dylan, for a magical sleigh ride around the village pond and a little way up Frog Hill. But not too far up and nowhere near Frog's Hollow. It was a Monday, after all.

'I bet the kids are having a fantastic time,' Christy said. 'But I was surprised they went so willingly with Hettie and Fred. Although I suppose as they think it's Father Christmas and his wife, nothing would've prevented them from going. And they love those reindeer to bits.'

'Sorry?' Cathy said, dragging her eyes from Leo's and smiling jubilantly at her friend.

Christy shook her head and rolled her eyes, glancing at Mia. 'I'm feeling a bit like a gooseberry. Look what this place has done to my best friend.' She was smiling though and Mia smiled back.

'Little Pondale is definitely a magical place. And there's no need for you to feel like a gooseberry. Bear's single now, and so is Toby.'

Mia winked at her as Ella handed Christy a sprig of mistletoe from a Christmas display on their table.

'And what am I meant to do with this? Go up and ask the single guys to kiss me?'

'That's what I would do,' Ella said, grinning.

'Hmm. I think I'll get another glass of wine instead. This is really kind of you to pay for everyone's drinks all night, Mia. I know you said you're rich, but even so. Some of these people look as if they've already emptied a barrel each.'

'At least they're having fun,' Mia said. 'That's what Christmas is about.'

'They won't be having fun when they wake up with a hangover,' Jet said, laughing. 'Especially as it's Christmas Day tomorrow. And poor Toby definitely isn't having a good time. I know Freda wanted to be with Alexia, but leaving Toby to hold the fort on Christmas Eve, is a bit much in my opinion. At least Alec should've stayed.'

'Or they should've hired more staff,' Gill added. 'Those two girls don't look as if they've worked behind a bar before.'

'They were the only ones available,' Lori said. 'Freda and Alec left everything until the last minute and trying to get bar staff at Christmas is like trying to find a golden goose.'

Christy smiled suddenly and tapped Cathy on her arm. 'Excuse me for a moment. I think I've got an idea. Will you look after Dylan for an hour or so?'

Cathy nodded, but she didn't take her eyes from Leo's face. 'Of course I will.'

'Then I'll go and do my good deed for the festive season and give that man a hand. It just so happens, I'm the best barmaid this side of the border. Even if I say so myself.'

Chapter Thirty-Six

There had been a change of plan for Christmas dinner. There were now even more people coming to Little Pond Farm on Christmas Day. So many people in fact that Jet had had to bring another table into the dining room as sixteen places weren't enough. It had increased from the eight originally planned, of Mia, Jet, Ella, Gill, Lori and Franklin and Hettie and Fred, to include Jenny and Glen, Cathy, Daisy and Leo, and Christy, Dylan and Toby. Jet had also invited Bear, because Jet didn't want him to be on his own. Not that it seemed he would be.

'Bear's bringing one of the barmaids from the pub last night,' Jet said, as he hung up the landline phone early on Christmas morning. The one beside his bed. 'That's okay, isn't it?'

Mia smiled and kissed him. 'Of course it is. It's your house and you can invite who you want. And one more won't make much difference.

Although how we're going to cook enough turkeys to feed them all is still beyond me. Gill says it'll be fine, because we can also use the outdoor oven. I didn't even know you had an outdoor oven.'

Jet grinned. 'That's because you still haven't been around the entire farm. We need to rectify that this week.'

'Hmm.' Mia quickly changed the subject. 'Did you hear Christy say that Toby had offered her a job in the pub while she's here?'

'Yep. Toby was really impressed with her skills. He told me so himself last night.'

Mia nuzzled Jet's neck. 'I don't think that's all he was impressed with. But she's supposed to be here on holiday, not to work in the pub. Mind you, from the way Christy and Toby were looking at one another, I'm pretty sure it won't be long before those two become an item. Quite how that's going to work once Cathy and Christy leave though, is anybody's guess. But miracles do happen, especially at Christmas.'

'Yes.' Jet wrapped his arms around Mia and pulled her closer. 'For example, Glen becoming the permanent incumbent of the parish church and vicarage of St Michael and All Angels.' He beamed at her and kissed her on the lips.

'Ah yes,' she replied, grinning broadly. 'It's surprising what a difference one phone call can make.'

'It's also surprising what a difference one day can make. Did you know that Cathy and Christy live in Milton Keynes? But that since coming here, Cathy's been seriously considering moving down this way. She was planning to look for somewhere to rent, in one of the nearby villages. Now that she's with Leo, that may change again.'

'I didn't know that. Do you think she'll go to London to live with Leo?'

Jet shrugged. 'I don't know. He asked me last night if I thought Sunbeam Cottage or Corner Cottage might be up for sale.'

Mia sat bolt upright. 'Did he?'

Jet nodded. 'I told him to ask you because you own them, but I didn't think you'd want to sell Sunbeam Cottage.'

She shook her head. 'I don't. I can't sell that. It was Mattie's. I don't think I could ever let that go.'

'Even if you no longer wanted to live there?' Jet gave her an odd look. 'I mean, if you had somewhere else you'd rather live?'

Mia smiled. Was this his way of saying that one day, in the dim and distant future, he might ask her to move in with him? Permanently, as opposed to just for the holidays.

'Even then. Ella and Gill might eventually live there. Or maybe Mum and Franklin.'

'That's what I thought.' He kissed her again and leapt out of bed. 'I'd better go and deal with the animals. I asked Gill and Franklin last night to give me a hand this morning. That way we'll get it done much sooner.' He strode towards the shower.

'Mum's going to be helping me and Ella in the kitchen, so take as long as you want. It may possibly get a bit chaotic in there. Although the trial run didn't go too badly. At least the vegetables were edible. And today, everything else will be too.' Mia scrambled out of bed and went to join Jet in the shower. 'This is going to be a wonderful Christmas, Jet.'

'It already is. Merry Christmas, Mia.'

'Merry Christmas, Jet.'

He pulled her into his arms and kissed her.

Several times.

Which meant he left later than he had said he was going to, to go and feed the animals and when Mia went out to tell him and Gill and Franklin to come inside for breakfast, she couldn't see them anywhere. They must have gone to one of the distant fields, which was exactly where Jet said they had been when they eventually came back.

Breakfast consisted of champagne, smoked salmon, scrambled eggs, and toast. Mia and Ella had cooked the eggs to perfection, which astonished Ella more than it did everyone else.

Then Jet told Mia he had a little surprise for her but it meant she had to go out. She was even more surprised when he told Little M to stay. Not that the dog seemed bothered. Having been out with Jet, Gill and Franklin, earlier Little M was happily getting to grips with the massive bone she'd just released from its Christmas wrapping.

Less than half an hour later, Mia was sitting in the sleigh, wrapped warmly in the fake fur blanket and Jet was taking her up Frog Hill, which, in spite of the gradient, the reindeer and sleigh were coping with without undue effort.

'Where are we going?' Mia asked.

'We're going to the Wishing Tree.'

'The Wishing Tree? Today? But, I've already made a wish. I came here with Ella on Sunday. Are you going to make a wish?'

Jet smiled at her but didn't say another word until at least five minutes later. 'I made a wish on Sunday, too, shortly after you and Ella, I believe. Now I want to see if mine will come true.'

Mia gasped as he stopped the sleigh. The Wishing Tree, which only had a few wishes adorned with coloured ribbons on it when she'd last seen it, was covered in myriad fairy lights and the branches were tied with white ribbon in amongst the other wishes and the dried, tan leaves still clinging on to the tree. A few small icicles hung here and there and the entire tree glistened and sparkled in the early morning sunlight as Jet lifted her down from the sleigh.

'Did you do this?' she asked, astonished by its beauty.

'Yes,' he said. 'With Gill and Franklin's help.'

'When?'

He grinned. 'After we'd fed the animals this morning. We were going to do it yesterday, but it was Monday, and none of us is foolish enough to come to Frog's Hollow on a Monday.'

She grinned back at him. 'It's gorgeous, Jet. But why?'

To her increased astonishment, he got down on one knee. 'Because I know how much you love trees adorned with Christmas lights.' His grin turned into a sexy, loving smile. 'And because I love you, Mia Ward. More than I thought it was possible to love someone. Because I've loved the last few days that you've been living in my house. Because you've made my house a home. And because I don't want you to leave after the holidays, or ever, for that matter. Because I want to share my life with you and for you to share yours with me. Because I want you to be Mrs Mia Cross. Because I want you to be my wife. Because I want you to marry me. Will you, Mia? Will you marry me?'

She blinked at him and shook her head in disbelief.

'Is that a no?' he croaked, looking as if his heart and soul had broken in two.

'God no, Jet!' she shrieked, throwing herself into his arms. 'It's a yes. A very definite *yes*! I was simply astonished, that's all. Are you sure this is what you want? Are you absolutely sure? I thought you were getting fed up with me being there. I thought you wished I would leave.'

He laughed and got to his feet, slipping the sparkling diamond ring onto the third finger of her left hand as she held it out to him.

'God, no,' he said. 'I was terrified you would leave. I decided on the very first night, that I wanted you to stay. I know it's early days for us, but I've never been more certain of anything in my life. I want you to be my wife. You are my forever, Mia. I love you with all of my heart.'

'And you are mine, Jet Cross. I love you with every fibre of my being. I can't wait to be your wife. Is this really what you wished for? Is this what you asked from the tree?'

He nodded. 'I asked that you would say yes to spending your life with me if I proposed.'

She threw back her head and laughed ecstatically. 'And I wished you would ask me to continue living with you at the farm. I was going to wish that you would propose, but I wasn't sure there was enough magic in the tree to ask for that.'

'Didn't Hettie tell you?' He furrowed his brows before beaming deliriously. 'The Wishing Tree will grant you anything, as long as you ask it nicely. And it'll do so within seven days, if it decides you're worthy.'

'Then thank heavens it thinks we're worthy. I love you, Jet. You've made me the happiest woman alive. This is the best Christmas present in the world. Ever.'

'Damn. I thought the books I've bought you were the best presents ever. They're called 'How to cook anything without blowing up a kitchen' and 'Everything you want to know about farm livestock but are afraid to ask.' Or something like that.' He grinned as she slapped his arm. 'I love you too,' he said, bending his head to kiss her. 'Merry Christmas, Mia.'

'Merry Christmas, Jet.' Mia grabbed the collar of his coat and pulled him towards her, impatient for his kiss. Their very first kiss as an engaged couple.

This was definitely the best Christmas Mia had ever had – so far.

MERRY CHRISTMAS!

Coming soon

Bells and Bows
on
Mistletoe Row

A Note from Emily

Thank you for reading this book. A little piece of my heart goes into all of my books and when I send them on their way, I really hope they bring a smile to someone's face. If this book made you smile, or gave you a few pleasant hours of relaxation, I'd love it if you would tell your friends.

I'd be really happy if you have a minute or two to post a review. Just a line will do, and a kind review makes such a difference to my day – to any author's day. Huge thanks to those of you who do so, and for your lovely comments and support on social media. Thank you.

A writer's life can be lonely at times. Sharing a virtual cup of coffee or a glass of wine, or exchanging a few friendly words on Facebook, Twitter or Instagram is so much fun.

You might like to join my Readers' Club by signing up for my newsletter. It's absolutely free, your email address is safe and won't be shared and I won't bombard you, I promise. You can enter competitions and enjoy some giveaways. In addition to that, there's my author page on Facebook and there's also a new Facebook group. You can chat with me and with other fans and get access to my book news, snippets from my daily life, early extracts from my books and lots more besides. Details are on the 'For You' page of my website. You'll find all my contact links in the Contact section following this.

I'm working on my next book right now. Let's see where my characters take us this time. Hope to chat with you soon.

To see details of my other books, please go to the books page on my website, or scan the QR code below to see all my books on Amazon.

Contact

If you want to be the first to hear Emily's news, find out about book releases, enter competitions and gain automatic entry into her Readers' Club, go to: https://www.emilyharvale.com and subscribe to her newsletter via the 'Sign me up' box. If you love Emily's books and want to chat with her and other fans, ask to join the exclusive Emily Harvale's Readers' Club Facebook group.

Or come and say 'Hello' on Facebook, Twitter and Instagram.

Contact Emily via social media:
www.twitter.com/emilyharvale
www.facebook.com/emilyharvalewriter
www.facebook.com/emilyharvale
www.instagram.com/emilyharvale

Or by email via the website:
www.emilyharvale.com

17509512R00162

Printed in Great Britain
by Amazon